I0822884

TRANSFORMED TAIL

A LITTLE MERMAID & FROG PRINCE RETELLING

DISPLACED FAIRYTALES

LEIALOHA HUMPHERYS

This book is a work of fiction. Any references to historical events, real people, or real places are used fictitiously. Other names, characters, places, and events are products of the author's imagination, and any resemblances to actual events or places or persons, living or dead, is entirely coincidental.

First paperback edition February 2026

ISBN (paperback) 978-1-959157-28-1

ISBN (ebook) 978-1-959157-27-4

ISBN (hardcover) 978-1-959157-29-8

Dust Jacket by GetCovers

Artwork by Jenelle Hovde

Published by Hokulani Press

Santaquin, Utah

United States of America

www.leialohahumpherys.com

To the ones who've never quite fit the mold.
To the wanderers, the in-betweeners, the ones who've felt too much or not enough.
You're not lost. You're on your way home.
This one is for you.

CHAPTER ONE
EZRA

The songbirds were dying, and if we didn't find a way to eliminate the pesky, invasive frogs, our whole island and ecosystem would crumble.

I could barely hear the birds as I dug my hands into the dirt, checking the texture, feeling if it was healthy soil in which to plant my *koa* trees. The terrace garden around me was carved into volcanic stone, with mist coiling through the ferns and other trees.

This is perfect. The soil was just ripe for planting. I stood, placed my *'o'o* stick into the ground, which made a little hole, as if someone had put their finger into the dark, nearly black dirt, then I placed a koa sapling into it.

The pack on my back was full of saplings, and I knew I had to hurry if I was going to get all of these planted before attending my next meeting.

A weight fell on my shoulders, and it wasn't the physical weight of the bag. It was the weight of being the soon-to-be-king of Kaiora Kingdom.

If only Tavo hadn't disappeared. I sighed.

Somewhere, in the distance, the high pitched croak of a

coqui frog broke the peaceful silence. I visibly cringed and looked in the direction of it. Much to my chagrin, I saw the little pest. He sat on the side of a tree, no larger than the tip of my finger. His bulgy black eyes stared at me, his golden brown skin glistened in the humid air, and his throat bubbled every few seconds. He would be rather cute if his presence wasn't killing the native birds.

The honeycreepers, the raptors, and flycatchers... They were all dying because of something this small, something that was multiplying and spreading faster than a wildfire.

With Tavo gone, the expectations on me pressed in. Courtiers wanted answers. The people wanted a cure to the frog infestation that killed hundreds of native birds and choked the forests with endless, deafening noise. And, mostly, father wanted me to step into shoes that did not feel like mine. Tavo had always trained to be king. Not me.

So much to do... so little time. I was only twenty four years old but I felt the responsibility of someone much older.

I rolled up my sleeves, my hands covered in soil, and made my way around the terraces, planting koa trees. I hadn't gotten far when someone spoke my name.

"Keoki."

I perked up and turned to see my father. So entrenched in my work, I hadn't heard his footsteps on the lava stone steps.

"Father." I quickly stood and bowed. How long had father been standing there? He looked every bit a king, with golden epaulets, a red sash around his waist, a dark tunic, and a red and yellow feather cape hanging from his neck. Wrinkles touched the corners of his eyes and his dark skin looked weathered, as if he'd spent more time outdoors than in the palace. He had aged since Tavo's disappearance.

We've all aged. I straightened out, trying to mask my grief with soberness.

"The council doesn't start for another hour–" I started to say when my father waved his hand.

"Are you hiding from the frogs or from the palace?" His tone, though serious, had a gentle undertone and there was a sparkle in his deep brown eyes.

I smiled wryly. "I think the frogs are winning."

"And what's your plan to conquer them?"

"Dig traps. Send out men every night to eradicate them..." I hated the thought of sending my troops out to the forest at night to listen for coqui frogs and kill any they found, but... we had gotten to this desperate point. It was all I could think of, my last resort that I would present to the council. We'd tried everything: traps and lures. And now... we had to go out at night and hunt them ourselves.

"You really think digging traps will work?" Father looked skeptical.

I sighed, feeling the heaviness on my shoulders again like a thousand pounds of lava rock. Was I disappointing him again with my lack of leadership? Did he think it was a bad idea, and that it would waste the time of our troops?

"I'm better at digging than diplomacy," I admitted and continued working, piercing the o'o stick into the ground and placing another koa tree into the hole.

Father walked over to me and crouched beside me, his eyes thoughtful as he scanned the area. "You know, when I was your age," he said, "I used to come here too. It wasn't a garden then... just lava rock and wild ferns." He motioned to a flat area on the highest terrace. "Years later, Tavo wanted to build a watchtower. You wanted to plan trees."

I smiled faintly, fingers threading through the dirt as I looked around us. From here, we could see the back of the palace, it's grand cream-colored pillars and arched windows, terracotta shingled rooves, and large windows standing out amongst the lush forest and fields around it.

And, beyond that, in the very far distance was the ocean. It was a faint blue, sparkling line from here, and a reminder that we were surrounded not just by our green island, but the sea... just a small drop in the much larger world of the Eight Seas.

"Tavo was meant to be king of all of this," I said. "Not me."

Without missing a beat, my father, the current king, spoke. "Whether Tavo took the throne or not, I would've pushed him to make peace." He eyed me. "But I don't worry with you."

I looked at him, unsure of what he meant. Father continued. "The island doesn't need another Tavo. It needs you, Ezra. Never doubt that."

Silence.

I wasn't sure how to answer. I could still remember the news, just months ago, that Tavo had been killed in foreign lands. They brought back his *leiomano,* his shark knife weapon, and, with tears in his eyes, father turned to me.

You will take Tavo's place as king. My stomach twisted like vines tangling itself up the sides of a tree. And, since the news, it seemed everything in Kaiora was turning against me: the frog infestation erupted, foreigners began coming in at unprecedented rates, plantations and immigrants were coming in from every corner of the Eight Seas, and it was all happening so fast, I felt like I had never had a chance to catch my breath.

And the people are angry at me. They demanded answers and solutions, and father gave me chances to step up. But I was failing, and it was crippling.

Moments like these were my only ones alone. Away from everyone, where I could finally breathe.

Except father was here, and though I loved him, I felt the immense pressure that he brought with him, always expecting me to do the right thing. To say the right thing. To come up with the right solutions.

I swallowed hard, eager to talk about something. Anything. It seemed like all father and I talked about were politics anyways. I felt silly for letting slip my insecurities.

"I've been studying the reports," I said. "The frogs are spreading faster in the Wailea forests, and the birds are fleeing to higher ground. Many of them can't survive up there for long because it's too cold. The foreigners are saying to bring in snakes."

My father frowned. "And risk worse? The last time we followed foreign advice, we lost half the honeycreepers."

Another bad mark. My stomach sank. Why did I even bring it up? I hadn't planned on bringing any snakes here, yet I didn't know what else to talk about with my father.

"So we stick to my plan?" I asked, my stomach knotting. "But what if that means devastating the land with our presence?" I could just imagine the damage that would be done if my armies stomped through the forest to hunt the coquis, one little frog at a time.

Father stood, brushing dirt from his palms, then said with firmness in his voice, "No. We listen. We pay attention to the *'aina,* as we have always done. We remember who we are." He looked up to the sky and added. "There's power in gentleness, Ezra. Don't let anyone tell you otherwise."

I wanted to hide, to pretend that father hadn't said that. Because he was, in essence, saying that *I* was gentle. I had never been powerful, commanding, or authoritative like

Tavo. I never ordered people around or asserted power or dominance.

And those were all things true leaders needed. I was too soft, too weak, too *gentle* to rule, and I hated it. I grit my teeth, wanting to tell my father I was going to try harder to be more like the man Tavo was.

But a messenger burst into the garden, a scroll clutched in his hand.

"Your majesty!" He bowed to the king and then to me. "A foreign ship has arrived."

I stood, my heart pounding. I had dreaded this day for weeks, knowing it would come at some point.

"The royal ship from Windmere has arrived," the messenger said, and nodded to me. "Princess Cressida is here."

My stomach sank. Princess Cressida, the young woman who was once betrothed to Tavo, was now here to sign betrothal papers to Kaiora's soon-to-be-king. Me.

For the hundredth time in my life, I just wished that Tavo was here and that the winds had not shifted this way.

CHAPTER TWO
AULANI

I darted between currents, feeling the water tugging at my hair, trying to pull me in its own direction, but I was stronger. Father would kill me for swimming near the surface, but had he ever swam against the current? It was exhilarating, and stole my breath away.

Humu, my little fish friend, had abandoned me waves ago, too scared to go as far as I'd gone.

I laughed as a pod of dolphins joined and circled me, smiles on their faces. They nudged their noses against me and clicked their tongues, and I could sense their approval of me. I mimicked them, playful and bright, as they burst above the surface, twirling and splashing. Spirals of light, reflections of rainbows, and dizzying glittering effects illuminated the surface. It was dazzling and amazing, and I wished we could stay in the sunlight forever.

My tail caught the sunrays, and I splashed beneath, noting that human ships were scattered like sea urchins along the horizon. I'd memorized their sails, their shapes and I know which ones fished, and which ones transported items.

Merchant ships, I told myself, remembering the conversation I'd overheard on board one of them.

Father would be so mad if he knew all the things I'd learned. I'd been sneaking onto the sides of ships for years, listening to the conversations of the sailors on board, dying to know more about the human world.

I'd never been caught. Perhaps there had been a few close encounters, but after all I'd learned, I could *not* stay away!

Why doesn't father see how fascinating their world is?

I passed a whale and smiled as it turned its body, leveling its eye with my face. Our minds connected, and I could feel its calm presence, like being in the ocean on a very still, quiet day.

Thank you. I rubbed my hand against its side, and began my dive into the deepness of the sea. I'd explored quite enough today, and if I tanned any darker, father would know I'd been spending more time in the sun than in the depths.

He'd tried everything to stop me from coming to the surface, including hiring some merfolk to follow me, but even they couldn't keep up.

As I descended, the sea grew darker and darker, and, it was once merfolk hit the very darkness, that we had to keep going. I hated this part, feeling as if the darkness consumed me, blinding me for only a moment. But once we passed through the darkness, the cold water became warm again and the underwater city appeared. Full of bioluminescent coral towers that glowed like lanterns, swirling seaweed gardens, kelp bridges that swayed like ribbons in the current, and pearl-covered dwellings, even I had to admit the Coral Realms was a sight to behold.

Fish of every color darted through open windows.

Music thrummed through the water in waves of vibration, like whalesong and heartbeat merged. Merfolk swam in graceful arcs: efficient, elegant, and habitual.

They often looked like fish with their pale skin, hair tinted in every color, and bright eyes. I darted through the streets, smiling and waving to those I passed.

"Slow down Aulani!" someone shouted, and another yelled for others to hear. "Watch out for the princess!"

"Always in a hurry," a mermaid huffed and scolded me but I hardly heard her. I had to get back to the coral castle, knowing my father wanted to meet with me.

"There you are!" Humu swam next to me, huffing as he attempted to keep pace. He had a thick black stripe around his eyes, with yellow coating the back part of his body and tail. I learned, by listening to human researchers, that they called Humu's type a wedge-tailed triggerfish.

"You should've come with me!" I laughed. He attempted to go around a pack of sardines, but I went straight through them. They opened a space for me to swim through, and Humu grudgingly followed.

"And get myself sucked in the current?" he asked. "No thank you. You're as reckless as those dolphins."

"If I could be a dolphin," I said, "I'd spend every day jumping above the surface like they do!"

As I moved through the hallways illuminated by giant glowing anemone, a figure waited outside the doors of father's court.

It was my older sister, Mo, short for Mohala. Her face was almost a mirror image of mine, but unlike me, her skin was fair. No freckles spotted her nose and cheeks, and instead of a reddish tint to her dark brown hair, she had a bluish tint. Instead of bright cerulean blue scales on her body, she had dark blue scales, and her tail was a colored combination of pinks and purples. I, on the other hand, had a bright rainbow colored tail.

"You were at the surface again, weren't you?" She asked, folding her arms.

I spoke lightly, a big smile on my face. "I didn't touch anything, Mo, and nobody saw me."

"Aulani." Mo's eyebrows furrowed. "Curiosity got the sea witch into trouble, and it'll do the same to you."

"You're sounding just like father." I looked from her to the closed doors, and understanding seeped in. "It's going to be bad, isn't it?"

"You must be obedient and respectful," Mo said, and her expression softened, like it always did when she was trying too hard to be stern. "I'm just worried for you, Au. You know that, right?"

I hugged my sister and she held me tighter than usual. A lump formed in my throat. What was father going to say now? Was he going to chain me to the depths? He had tried everything to keep me here, below the surface. What would he try today?

"I know, and I appreciate you for that." We parted and I held her shoulders. "I do love you, Mo. I just don't like being trapped down here."

She pursed her lips and tipped her head towards the door. "Good luck, Au."

I then went in, finding my father speaking with a wise old sea turtle. It turned its green head towards me and stared at me with his bright golden eyes.

I bowed, he tipped his head, then excused himself.

Now it was father, mother, and I, all alone in this room that was larger than the inside of a whale's mouth. Father sat on his throne, his golden triton in his hand, and a shining crown on his head. Even in his older age, he was a handsome man. His blue eyes sparkled and his gray beard and hair floated in the water.

Mother was also dazzling, with her dark hair pulled into a long braid decorated with starfish and glowing pearls.

My heart sank as father spared no effort in pleasantries. He got straight to the point, and I rather appreciated that about him.

"You are hereby *forbidden* from going to the surface. Do you understand me, Aulani Laniakea?"

Oh no. He was using my full name.

I opened my mouth to speak but when he lifted his triton, I immediately pursed my lips together. When he lifted that, someone could get hurt. And I most certainly didn't want it to be me.

Father was a good ruler of the Coral Realms, but he did use his powerful triton to enforce the rules, especially the one about magic. He *despised* anyone who used magic except himself, because magic was difficult to control. He said the triton controlled magic, and those who tried to use it without a tool risked unimaginable woes on the merfolk.

That triton though... I stared at its golden tips, the way it seemed to glow. Father had used the triton on people who disobeyed him. He turned them to coral, seaweed, and, sometimes, even jellyfish–helpless to the currents and tides.

He'd transform them back, of course, but he'd never used that triton on me. I was his daughter, and the youngest, after all...

Sometimes he used the triton's powerful beams to destroy things. I even saw him command a group of fish to swarm a merfolk's home. The triton did, indeed, possess magic that I did not understand, nor did I care to understand. I felt magic, the tingling sensation in the water, and I was glad it was one less thing to worry about.

Gives me more time to explore and take care of the royal gardens...

Father's words cut my thoughts short. "I have arranged a betrothal between you and King Malinoakea of the Brine."

I gaped. "Father–"

Mother's eyes hardened and before he could speak, she did. "Aulani, you have disrespected and disobeyed your father for far too long. You will be grateful he even secured you a marriage. Your rebellious reputation has spread far and wide, and you have no idea the lengths we went to get an agreement for marriage."

My heart sank. "I'm sorry," I said, and I really meant it. I knew my parents loved me, and I wanted to be grateful. I had a good life... but there was just a part of me that couldn't stay here. I was dying to know what was out there: how the humans studied the stars, the things they created, the technology, the walking on land...

My stomach tightened. *But I'm a mermaid.* I looked at my parents. "Were there no other prospects? King Malinoakea lives in the deepest part of the sea–he eats whale bones for dinner and never surfaces for light." I thought I'd stop breathing. "Not to mention he's thousands of years old. I'd be his what? His sixtieth wife? I'm only twenty-two years old–"

"Aulani!" My mother cut in. "You should be grateful to be marrying someone who takes care of this ocean. Unlike the humans you idolize, Malinoakea ensures our oceans remain clean. There's so much that goes on in the brine."

I knew this. The ocean floor fish and merpeople were unlike any others, with eyes that could see in the dark and lights in their tails that didn't need rays from the sun to shine.

"But it's so..." My voice cracked. "It's so dark down there."

Before either of my parents could respond, a rush of words came out like a tsunami. "What about Prince Eryn from the Pearl Realms? He might be vain, yes, but he's not in the depths of the sea. Or what about the noblemerman from the icy parts in the north? It would be cold, yes, but I could handle it–"

"Your sisters have been offered a hand in marriage by these choices," said father. "But you, Aulani... There is no hope. The merfolk know what you are: a human lover. Human seeker." He looked disgusted, and a lump formed in my throat.

"I just think there's so much they can–"

"Silence!" Father rose from his seat. "You have dishonored me too many times. You *will* marry Malinoakea. Furthermore, between now and your marriage–which will be in one month's time–you are *forbidden* from ever going to the surface, here *or* in any realm."

"And if you try again," father added. "Your punishment *will* be severe."

I frowned. What did they have planned?

"The triton can create a barrier," mother said and my whole body froze. "It's what keeps the veil of darkness over our beloved realm, so the outside world cannot see us until they pass through it."

Understanding seeped in, like squid ink blackening the water. They were going to create a barrier *just* for me, one that would keep me below the ocean's surface.

Father's gaze hardened, and I knew he would do this if he had to.

He'd done it for one other mermaid in the kingdom, and she could not break the surface.

I nodded, but my heart was racing. I had to get away. There were no words.

I bowed, and swam out, darting past Humu, who sighed and asked, "What now Aulani?"

But he wouldn't understand.

Nobody would.

Nobody... except her.

I swam through the coral forests, past illuminated jellyfish, and into the darkest corner of the realm.

To others, this lair was dark and ominous, but to me, it was warm and strange. As I swam in, I was greeted by cracked seashells, swirling sand pools, driftwood shelves full of jars, and bioluminescent jellyfish floating around.

"Aunty Lorelei?" I hadn't reached her when the tears started pouring.

"Oh dear." My aunt quickly pulled me into her arms. We weren't actually related, but she felt like a dear aunt. Her skin was the color of ash, and her hair a dark brown with an emerald tint. Her scales were green and her tail was a dazzling iridescent display of green and gold. Since she had been under the sea for so long, her skin turned an unnatural gray color. To others, she was quite terrifying to look at. To me, she was safe. "What happened?" She stroked my hair and I cried. I sobbed as I shared what had just happened.

"You're to be wed?" Aunty Lorelei sounded more shocked at that than my impending prison.

"I'm going to be caged in." Fresh tears blended into the saltwater around us. "And I don't want to marry King Malinoakea. He keeps his people and his wife trapped on the sea floor." More tears.

"I just want to run away," I admitted. "I'm so tired of this, and father lifted his triton." It felt like my insides were being squeezed at the thought of being under father's wrath. "I just want to see the human world," I said. "I want to learn. I want to read. I want to explore the land. Climb their mountains. Feel their fresh water. I don't want to be stuck here anymore."

"You don't have to run away to belong." Aunty Loralei's voice was calm and soothing as a sea harp singing the ocean to sleep. She stroked my hair. "You can stay, use your gifts, love bravely, and be exactly who Akua made you to be — both ocean and land, past and future."

"I'll be happier if I leave," I said quietly. My aunt's gaze softened, her green eyes shining like the sun on the lush mountains in the distance. I could feel the weight of her years in those eyes, the quiet sorrow of someone who had once wanted more but had been bound by magic.

"I wanted that too, when I was younger," she said. This is why I loved her. She'd told me many stories, and the risks she took to even *walk* on land, to shed her tail and have legs even for one day. That very action had made her an outcast, but she seemed to have seen *everything* there. And now she was trapped here, just like me.

When father found out she'd created a potion that allowed her to walk on land, *and* she used magic to aid with that potion, he imprisoned her here... just as he was going to do to me if he ever found out I went to the surface again. My heart seized up at that thought. I loved my adopted aunt, but I didn't want to be trapped here like her. And she understood that.

"Aulani," she said, her tone soft but knowing. "I see the fire in you, the same fire I once had. But that world *is* dangerous. There are things humans do that you will never understand." She smiled gently. "You should listen to your father's counsel. It's safer down here."

I wiped my eyes and nodded, but I couldn't help looking past my aunt to her driftwood shelves with jars of strange items and potions. An idea entered my mind, one so forbidden and dangerous, I did not have the courage to say it aloud to my aunt.

But she seemed to understand anyway. "No, Aulani. I will *not* make you a potion to walk on land."

"But I don't belong here," I pleaded. At that, she gently pushed me away.

"Go home, sweet girl. I love you, but I will not entertain that."

I grabbed my hair in frustration.

I loved my aunt. I loved my parents and my family... but... *I have to leave.* If I didn't, I'd be imprisoned in the Brine, sweeping up the ocean floors, feeding on whale bones, and living in darkness for the rest of my days.

No... I could not fathom it. I had to get out.

CHAPTER THREE
EZRA

The royal garden was all order and symmetry: tiny hedges, prim fountains, and swan ponds lined with marble tiles. I always felt like a guest in it, not a gardener nor an owner. The roses here didn't bloom wild. They obeyed. There weren't even any native plants here–no plumerias, hibiscus, ti leaves, not even a gardenia. Tavo had put together this garden, because he wanted the foreigners to feel like home when they came to our palace.

I glanced behind me at the terrace garden behind the palace, waterfalls pouring out of crevices in the mountain, and the lush, chaotic forest that came from it. Just yesterday I was there, planting koa trees. And after that meeting with my father, the council had been intense. I somehow persuaded them to let the armies hunt the coqui frogs.

They'd gone out last night, and reported killing *hundreds* of frogs. We burned the frog remains that morning, and I grimaced at the thought. I hated *killing* things, but this was a necessary step. If there was ever a bad time to be a frog in Kaiora Kingdom, it was now.

My attention turned to the clicking of my companion's slippers on the stone ground. The princess of Windmere had spent the night at the palace, but now we were officially meeting. Cressida held my arm, her parasol in her other gloved hand, her eyes focused on the path ahead. She was the picture of restraint: her pastel-blue gown cinched at the waist, its corseted bodice boned with pearl-studded seams. Pale blonde hair glinted like polished silver under the sun, and when she looked up at me with her icy blue eyes, they had a distant look to them.

We had strolled through the garden for a while, and neither of us could seem to find any words to speak. My meetings exhausted me that day, and her journey seemed to exhaust her. Yet here we were, fulfilling our political obligations.

We had just signed betrothal papers. But I didn't even want to think about *our* marriage. She probably didn't want to think about it either. It was awkward, really.

She was the youngest princess in the Windmere family, a spare.

Just like me. That should've helped us find some solidarity, but I couldn't help feeling her bitterness. She had visited twice and courted Tavo, not me. But with him gone, and her being the "spare" princess, her father quickly sent her here to sign new betrothal papers to marry me.

I thought about declining to sign the papers but my counselors advised me otherwise. "This is the role of a monarch," said one of them. "Marriage alliances strengthen foreign ties, open doors to new allies, and improve our political and economic trade."

So, with no thought of myself or my feelings, I signed the papers.

I'd never imagined a romantic marriage–never really

allowed myself to think of it anyway... because I was the spare. I'd do whatever Tavo ordered me to do when he became king.

Cressida let go of my arm to pull something from her dress.

A golden ball? It glinted like sunlight trapped in metal, a perfect orb that didn't belong here. I frowned. "That's new." The first words spoken between us.

She turned it in her palm, her expression unreadable. "I bought it from a woman in Windmere. She said the person who retrieves it for me is a true prince."

I raised an eyebrow. Was she going to throw it and expect me to chase after it like a dog? The idea was quite offensive.

"Can I see?" I asked, and she handed it to me. I read the writing around the center band of the ball. "A kiss from a true princess will break any spell." I frowned. What was she implying? Was she suggesting that her kiss might break some "spell?" Then my stomach tightened. Was the "spell" her feelings for Tavo?

I turned it around, finding more writing. "Beware. True magic always takes something in return."

Magic. I handed it back to her. "There's no magic in Kaiora," I said. It wasn't illegal to use magic, as there were some who practiced kahunaism and witchcraft. But magic just wasn't at work here.

"That's interesting," I said. "Why'd you get it?"

Her fingers tightened slightly on the orb and I felt a strange pressure in the air, like a charged, quiet moment before a lightning storm. Nervousness flooded me as she glanced at my lips.

Did she want to kiss me? Is that why she got the ball? To instigate a kiss?

I hadn't ever kissed a girl, and I wasn't quite in the mood to kiss Cressida. She was agreeable, but I had never viewed her as, well... my companion. My wife.

Might as well start now, I told myself, but I couldn't do it. Not when I'd seen her and Tavo all over each other in the past. I suppose marriage, to me, was going to be nothing romantic. Just a duty for my people. This whole situation was making me rather nauseated.

"I know this wasn't what either of us expected," she said, avoiding eye contact. "Tavo was supposed to marry me. We had so many plans together, and now..." She shook her head. "He..." She paused and I thought she would say, "Die" or "was killed."

Instead, she said, "He never came back." She sounded more angry at the fact he never returned than that he had died, which was strange. "You were supposed to do your own thing, Ezra. You weren't ever supposed to be the heir."

My fist clenched, and my jaw tightened. What was she getting at? Did she see me as inferior to Tavo too?

Probably.

We reached the side of the garden, which connected it to the terrace garden. Ponds glistened in the sunlight, and blossoms floated across their surface. Cressida's reflection hovered in the water.

"I'm not Tavo," I said. "Though I'll try to be more like him."

"No." Cressida finally looked at me. "You're not Tavo. But I don't think you could ever be like him either." For the first time, I wondered if there might be some truth to her words.

Father said it.

Cressida said it.

Was I putting too much pressure on myself to be like

him, when that could never be a reality? It made me sick with worry.

But Cressida watched me with curiosity, and I wondered, maybe even allowed myself to entertain the idea of becoming friends. She'd always been obsessed with Tavo, but now that he was gone, could I put myself in that position? The position that was once his?

"I'm sorry you and Tavo couldn't be together," I said.

"Me too." She pursed her lips, then added. "But I can carry on his legacy in my own way."

People grieved in their own way and I figured this was her way of grieving Tavo. But what legacy of his did she mean? Tavo hadn't even been king yet. Had never made any laws or decrees. He often seemed indifferent to the whereabouts of the kingdom. So what legacy of his was there to carry on, besides his dominating and powerful personality?

Cressida held up the ball, but instead of handing it to me, it slipped from her fingers and fell into the pond. Her eyes flicked towards it, then to me.

"What a loss," she said, the golden ball invisible in the deep pond. Did she expect me to get it? I wasn't afraid of getting wet, but... something seemed off.

"I can get it," I finally decided before I changed my mind. Before things got too awkward. I took my shoes off, and as soon as my foot touched the water, something happened. I could see the ball from here, at the bottom of the pond, with bright orange and white koi fish swimming back and forth.

The ball pulsed once, then glowed bright as lightning.

And suddenly...

Cressida screamed. I didn't understand; the world around me grew larger and larger. A burning sensation waved through my chest. My muscles wrenched. Everything spiraled. I dropped–no, collapsed, my limbs curling inward, my hands gone.

I hit the pond, and water swallowed me. Breathing felt impossible. Moving felt unnatural. The garden above warped and shimmered.

The last thing I saw through bulging, panicked eyes was Cressida's silhouette above the water, one hand over her mouth, and the golden ball, with drops of water sparkling on it, in the other.

Then she ran away.

CHAPTER FOUR
AULANI

The sea was alive tonight, its motions and currents restless.

Or perhaps it was me. I couldn't stop thinking about my father's new rule. Word had spread throughout the Coral Realm of my betrothal to King Malinoakea and while everyone congratulated me, even they looked sorry.

They knew, as well as I, that he would imprison me there. In his dark abyss, surrounded by ghostly shipwrecks and mermaids with skin the color of ash.

I'll never get to see the sun.

I tried to entertain the idea of exploring the shipwrecks, but...

It'd be so dark. Why didn't the king of the Brine marry someone from his own kingdom, someone who could already see in the darkness?

I swallowed hard, tossing back and forth in my seaweed bed.

My sisters all slept soundly, but couldn't they sense that the sea was moving? It was alive and raging... Or perhaps it was me.

I sat up.

If I go to the surface one last time, I will give myself closure, I decided. Yes. That was a good idea.

One. Last. Time. I moved past my sisters with a stealth that even an octopus would envy. But Mo stirred.

"Au? Is that you?"

"Yes, I'm just getting... something to drink." I smiled sweetly, and she closed her eyes, waving her hand at me as if I disrupted her. When I reached the door, little Humu was there, like he'd been waiting for me.

"Humu?"

"There you are Aulani! I was wondering if you'd lost your connection with the sea," he teased, his fishy lips always looking so silly when he spoke.

"Shh..." I looked back at my sisters, though they were still sleeping, then closed the door. Guards would be everywhere, but I knew just the places to get out.

"There's something happening up there," Humu said quietly. "Something's wrong."

"I can sense it." I nodded, and we left the castle together.

The entire underworld kingdom was asleep, the lights all dimmed, the pods and clams closed up, and even the seaweed curled for the night.

As we passed through the dark veil, I couldn't help but feel as if it was grabbing my body, trailing its darkness across every inch of my skin.

I will be imprisoned... No sun. No waves. No humans. I'd be stuck here forever if father found out I went to the surface again...

This will be the last time, I promised.

Before we reached the surface, I could see the waves breaking against the water, the entire world a swirling white chaos. The current pulled stronger than I'd ever felt it.

When I broke the surface, a storm surged above. Thunder clapped across the sky. Lightning ripped through.

A ship creaked and groaned as merciless waves pounded it. Its sails ripped like dry seaweed and the mast crumbled like brittle coral. Splintered wood sank into the deep. I could make out several dinghies full of men, and my heart relaxed a little. Yet, they were calling out for someone.

"Prince Ryker! Prince Ryker!"

A prince?

Oh no. My heart stammered. Where was their beloved prince? They sounded so sad as they called out for him.

Before I could even nose around for the prince, the ship exploded. It was so loud and frightening; I darted beneath the waves like a scared fish.

Humu screamed as he dodged the falling wreckage. I moved aside from a beam and swam through the debris like a maze, hoping I might help find their prince.

And that is when I saw him. The man was not much older than me, barely clinging to a broken beam. Fire and smoke filled the surrounding area, and I hesitated.

He's human.

But I can't just let him die! The dinghies were already heading towards the lighthouse shining in the distance. They still called out for their prince, but it became more and more distant.

He would die if I left him here on this beam. The beam could sink, or he would lose his grip, or... a million other things.

I made up my mind and ignored Humu, who screamed we should probably go. I grabbed the prince just as he slipped from the beam. With my hands under his arms, his weight suddenly dragged me down.

I broke through the surface, allowing the back of his head to rest on my shoulder as I kicked towards shore.

I avoided the dinghies because I wouldn't be so reckless to reveal myself to them. Saving this man's life was going to get me in enough trouble if anyone found out.

Dragging his heavy, muscular frame through the water labored my breaths and made my whole body ache by the time I reached shore. When I got him onto the sand, I took a moment to catch my breath, then rested my head on his chest to check for a heartbeat.

He's alive! Rain continued to pour, and lightning lit up the scene: a lonely beach with a mermaid and human prince.

I looked down at his face, wiping dripping rainwater from it. He was handsome, with dark hair and tanned skin. His frame showed he was familiar with hard labor and physical work, an attribute that I admired.

The prince wore a jacket, but the ordeal had torn it up yet... something caught my eye. It poked out of his pocket, and I could barely make out the golden gleam in the darkness.

My heart skipped a beat as I examined it.

A telescope. I'd seen the sailors hold this up to their eyes, and I could only imagine what they saw because of it. I'd also seen some people on top of the castle using it to study the stars. Exhilaration pulsed through me.

I have to see the stars through the telescope. I decided to take a look, but the prince's breathing slowed, and I sensed he was fading away.

No... Raising my voice, I sang.

E hiamoe, e hiamoe,

The tide has found you, soft and slow.
The stars above still know your name,
Even when you've lost your way.

E ho'omālie, no need to fear,
The sea carries you home from here.
I'll sing until breath returns to stay,
And all your sorrow drifts away.

The melody rippled through the water, as if telling it to calm down. I'd always been aware of the way my song could calm the world around me.

As if in response, the storm ended. Songbirds tweeted from the nearby forest. The melody echoed in the wind and it ignited a frequency. The prince's breathing steadied.

I smiled softly, and that is when his eyes opened. It was so unexpected, so sudden, I gasped, dropped the telescope, and splashed into the water without a word. Humu dashed after me. When we were a safe distance, we watched.

The sea-washed prince rubbed his head and looked around.

Prince Ryker. I said his name in my mind, thinking about the telescope, and conjuring up a plan...

I have to walk on land, I thought. There was no other way. No other escape from my impending marriage. I would do whatever it took.

With that, I swam straight to the sea witch's lair.

Before I reached the deepest part of the cave, my aunt appeared, a glowing jellyfish lighting the lair.

"The answer is no," she said, her arms folded.

"You've felt it though, haven't you?" I asked. "The ache. The pull. I don't belong down here. I *must* learn. I have more to give up there."

"Curiosity is not the same as calling, child."

"But what if it is? What if Akua gave me this curiosity on purpose? What if I'm *meant* to be up there?"

Silence.

My aunt looked at me, her eyes full of sorrow I could not explain. My heart squeezed in my chest. What if she said no? Where would I go? Would I have to run away, far, *far* from here in order to escape? Was there another sea witch or sorcerer who might help me?

But Aunt Lorelei was all I knew, and I sometimes wondered if her use of magic–something no other mermaids used besides my father–was underestimated.

The woman stared into my eyes, and I silently pleaded, hoping she would understand.

"There is a potion," she finally said. "It won't last forever. You will need to win the right prince's heart to stay."

"I don't want a prince," I said, but then I immediately regretted it. I had to take any options.

The sea witch began turning her back and I quickly shot back. "Wait! I mean..." I thought about Ryker. What if... What if I got *him* to fall in love with me? I could be a princess in *their* world, and, as princess, learn and travel and do *everything* I could ever want!

Yes! This solution was more perfect than a dolphin catching a wave.

"I will win the right prince's heart," I said. "I just met him tonight."

She raised an eyebrow, but nodded. “These things are risky, Aulani,” she said. “But this is how the potion works.” She motioned for me to follow her deeper in her lair, her green-tinted hair floating behind her. “The potion gives you legs for one month. If, within that month you win the heart of the right prince for you, you will stay a human forever.”

The thought thrilled me, and I gasped. “Yes–”

“Wait.” She moved towards her driftwood shelves and began picking out items. “There is a price.”

“What is it? I’ll pay for it.”

“Your voice or your past.”

I frowned. My past? No. I couldn’t give up everything I learned, loved, and all the memories with my family. No. I couldn’t do that.

But my voice? How would I communicate with the prince? What about singing to the birds and life of the land and sea? I would deeply miss being able to communicate with them!

I can do it though. Through actions, especially because I could not read or write, I was sure I could get the prince to fall in love with me!

I hesitated, then nodded. “My voice. I can live without it.” Then I quickly added. “Will I get it back if I win the prince’s heart?”

My aunt nodded solemnly, then retrieved a small glowing vial of blue. My heart raced. Was the answer to walking on land here all along?

“I love you, Aulani.” She gently touched my cheek, and I could see she was crying. “I wish it didn’t have to be this way.” And it was then I realized... I would never see my aunt again. Because if I succeeded, I wouldn’t swim all the way to this underwater world. And because my aunt was imprisoned down here, she could not come to the surface to see me.

The tears flowed from my own eyes as I hugged her goodbye. I wished she could feel my deep gratitude for all she'd done for me and been to me.

And now, she was giving me the chance to take my life into my own hands. I wouldn't be confined to the deepest part of the sea.

The potion was warm in my hand, the liquid swirling with an otherworldly blue glow. It was everything I had hoped for. This would allow me to leave the ocean, to walk on land as a human, to experience the world I had only seen from the surface of the water.

Finally!

My aunt's words echoed in my mind, ones she'd spoken before: *You don't have to run away to belong.* I quickly dismissed it.

"Thank you, thank you!" I said, and Aunt Lorelei held me tight before letting go.

"Hurry, child," she said.

As I reached the mouth of the lair, I froze.

Someone was there. Waiting for me.

"Mo?"

Humu swam faithfully beside me, a nervous look on his face.

Mohala paled when she saw me, her eyes darting from me to the potion in my hand.

Mo had always been the one who understood me best, the one who never called me strange or freakish, the one who had always smiled when I expressed my yearn for something more. Yes, she scolded me too, even when she understood.

But now I wasn't so sure.

Fear clouded her eyes, like murky water after a storm.

"Aulani." Her voice trembled. "What is that?" She pointed at the blue, glowing vial.

"It's my choice, Mo," I said. "I can't marry the man of the brine."

My heart sank, sensing the shift in my sister's gaze.

"No," Mohala interrupted, her voice sharp, almost panicked. "You don't understand what you're doing. Once you drink that, you'll be..." Her voice cracked. "You'll be lost to us. Gone."

"I won't be gone. I'll still be me. The world out there is waiting for me. Besides, I don't fit here, Mo. I've never fit in, and you know that. But in the human world... maybe I could belong."

My sister's face twisted in anguish, and she swam forward. "You don't belong there, Aulani! You don't know what that world is like. They'll hurt you. They'll see you as a thing, a *monster!* Don't throw everything away! Stay with us!"

The words hit me like a wave crashing against the rocky cliffs. I wasn't naïve.

I wasn't just *throwing my life away.* The human world called to me, and there I would learn. Grow. Explore. But Mo's fear twisted in my chest like a cruel knot, tightening the more she spoke.

"I understand you better than anyone," Mo said, and straightened out, steely resolve in her eyes. "That's why I can't let you make this mistake, Au."

Before I could reply, Mo's eyes flickered to something behind me, a shadow lurking on the edge of the rocks that made up Aunty Lorelei's lair. I turned just in time to see our mother, her face edged with stone coldness, and my father, now appearing tall and imposing, his triton in hand. His eyes narrowed at me as if he already knew what had happened.

My heart stopped.

Mo betrayed me. The moment I had waited for all my life... and Mo betrayed me. My parents hadn't just found out–they had been *waiting* for me to slip up. They knew I'd leave. They knew I'd go to the surface, and they knew Mo would tell them.

"It wasn't just you who was going to get into big trouble," Mo said through tears.

She'd been waiting outside the doors to the throne room that day... because my parents spoke to her first.

She betrayed me. It was all I could think of, my breaths short, my mind working itself into a frenzied panic.

"Aulani." Father's voice was like thunder, the weight of his authority falling on me now. "You will not disgrace our family like this. You will stay, and you will accept your place next to the king of the brine."

Couldn't breathe. I knew what was coming, especially as his golden triton lit up.

"You *will* stay," he said, his voice filled with finality.

I glanced at Mo. Guilt and fear filled her face; I had never seen that kind of fear in her before. The world shifted around me, the ocean's gentle sway turning into something darker, heavier.

Magic....

There was no time to explain. There was no time to convince them that I had set my heart or that my calling–this destiny–was beyond the sea.

I had to go. I had to flee.

Without a word, I swam as fast as I could towards the surface. "Don't hurt her!" I could hear Humu behind me, risking his life to distract my father.

"Stop her!" The king's voice boomed throughout the water. It felt as if the water turned against me.

Just like swimming against a current, I told myself, pushing through. But my father's magic was stronger.

"No!" another voice screamed.

Aunt Lorelei!

And suddenly the current's pull lessened. Magic bubbled around me, golden from my father and emerald from... Aunt Lorelei? Water whizzed past me as I pushed to the surface, potion in hand. Once I reached the shore and turned human, father could not touch me.

I'm so close.

The surface neared, moonlight breaking through the clouds above.

And that was when the surrounding water shimmered... then *shifted,* like it was moving, getting displaced by some other water...

I gasped.

The ocean turned icy. Heavy. Salt vanished from my senses, and I felt a tug unraveling in my chest.

This isn't the ocean.

And then light. Blinding. Piercing.

Cold air. Fresh air.

I burst from the water... and everything was wrong.

Gray skies. Thick, lush trees. Misty mountains and waterfalls like cliffs around me. The warm salty winds were gone, as were the waves.

And there was nobody following me. I was not in the sea anymore. I clutched my shoulders and looked around, the sound of something croaking in the distance.

Tears fell from my already fear-stricken face. "Where am I?"

CHAPTER FIVE

EZRA

Days turned into weeks. Maybe months.

Not only did I lose track of time, but I felt I was losing my mind. Each day as a frog made me feel less and less like my human self and more and more like I was permanently turning into the creature I vowed to destroy.

This was the true game of survival: a constant pursuit of bugs to eat, of safe places to rest. Of running from frog catchers.

I couldn't even remember what it felt like to stand, even less to talk. Anytime I heard a human voice, my instinct was to flee, not to listen. So I had no idea how much time had elapsed or what conversations I might overhear on the whereabouts of my kingdom, the throne, the villages, anything.

The words on the ball continued to plague my mind: A kiss from a true princess will break any spell.

It was all I could think about, all I could hope for.

But where? How? There were no princesses in Kaiora kingdom... besides Cressida... and was she even looking for me? Did she realize what happened? My memories were fleeing, as if my small frog brain struggled to latch onto my human mind–wherever that mind might be.

And yet, somehow... I still hoped. Still fought, because if I didn't fight for my kingdom and for my survival, who would? I don't know what kept me going from month to month, day to day, minute to minute...

But perhaps it was my kingdom, and the fact that if I disappeared, who would rule them? Would the foreigners come in? Had they already come? Because one day, the frog catchers stopped.

Disappeared.

And everywhere I went, I found myself hopping away–running away from other frogs. They looked at me with their big black eyes, their slick greenish yellow skin, and I knew they would attack me if I didn't leave.

I was not one of them, and never would be.

If there was one thing I didn't want to lose, it was my humanity. Even if I felt it fading from me with each passing day.

Someone was splashing. Violently. Loudly. Over and over. It was the most noise I'd heard up here since becoming one of these disgusting little coquis, and it startled me. Was it a frog hunter that came up this far? Why were they splashing like that then?

I climbed up the side of the tree, internally cursing when I involuntarily let out a loud *coqui!*

Wretched frog form... How long had I been like this? The days turned into weeks and I lost track in my will to survive. After Princess Cressida screamed, she ran away, and I swam out of the pond, calling after her, begging for help. But she had disappeared, and I knew I was in more danger than anything.

Frog hunters were all over the gardens, and the involuntary *ribbit* sounds that exhibited themselves as high pitched, incredibly annoying "coqui!" were spilling out of my mouth like hiccups. One of the frog hunters spotted me and came running towards me, net in hand.

I screamed and leaped away as fast as I could. To this moment, I was sure I only survived through divine intervention. I managed to climb up the terrace–or, rather, *hopped*–then tracked into the highest and deepest parts of the forest, where the waterfalls and freshwater ponds were as plentiful as the sands on the sea. The frog hunters were up here for days on end, and I had to keep moving in order to hide from them.

I'd had too many close encounters. I'd learned to stay in areas that were very dense in brush, somewhat filtered by the noise of the waterfalls and water, and cold. I was dying, really, in the cold, but there were fewer coquis that dared come this far, and, therefore, fewer bullying frogs.

But lately, there had been no signs of frog hunters.

Either they'd given up going this far, or the royal decree to eradicate all the frogs had come to a halt. It gave me hope that my father had gotten word of what had become of me. Yet so many questions remained: did Cressida see me turn into a frog? And, if so, wouldn't she have told my father? Wouldn't he come looking for me if he knew that?

It was awfully exhausting to think through all of it, especially with my doubts creeping up. What if father didn't care to come after me? Perhaps he thought I was weak to fall prey to any kind of magic, something that was foreign to our island, or maybe Cressida really didn't see me transform?

After all, when I came out of the water and called after her, she just ran away. Did she even hear me talking, or was I just making a "coqui" noise without realizing it?

More questions pounded in my tiny amphibious brain: how did I turn into a frog? Who turned me into a frog? Did someone curse me? Was it Cressida? Or did someone hide in the garden that day I turned to a frog?

In any event, I was alive. And now I had to figure out this noise, or I might get surprised by a coqui hunter.

As I peered over the branch into the pond below, I gaped. The first thing I saw was the rainbow tail, connected to a scaly bright blue body. The tail dazzled in shades of reds and pinks, blending to rich orange, sunshine yellow, bright green, sea blue, indigo, and finally vibrant violet at the tips of the tail. It was beautiful and breathtaking, but what caught my breath and made me gape, even as a frog, was that the top half of this thing... this *fish* body was a *person.* No...

A mermaid. I'd heard of mermaids before. They were the stuff out of fairy tales. Some people said that mermaids used to live in our waters thousands of years ago, but they became extinct by choosing to walk on land. Nobody believed they were actually real, including myself.

Until now. This was a mermaid, no doubt about it.

She had olive-tanned skin, with a light blue, mesh blouse covering her top. And her dark brown hair... *Whoa.*

I blinked.

Hints of red in her hair dazzled in the sunlight filtering through the trees. I watched, too mesmerized, terrified, and amazed all at the same time to do anything... until.

Coqui! Coqui! Coqui! It was like my racing, amazed heart was setting off the ribbit-ing. The thrashing suddenly stopped. The mermaid looked around, alarmed, and then her eyes settled in my direction.

"Who's there?" she asked, shivering. "I can hear you, and sense you. Where are you?" At that, she came closer to the tree I hid in.

Stop coqui-ing! I chastised myself, but the frog body had a mind of its own. It kept going in a panicked frenzy.

And that was when the mermaid saw me. Compared to my size, she was very large. I was only about the size of her eye, if that, yet the way she looked at me made me feel like... she would not hurt me.

"Are you alright there?" she asked through chattering teeth, her arms wrapped around her shoulders.

"Yes," I squeaked, and she jumped, causing cold water to splash on me.

"You can talk?"

"Of course." I frowned, and the concern on her face loosened, turning into a beautiful, gentle smile. I gaped. The freckles on her cheeks were visible, and so were the golden flecks in her big brown eyes. Her hair smelled like saltwater, and her skin was sun-kissed, like she spent hours on a beach. Unlike the tight curls of the foreigners or the loose waves of the islanders, her hair was a mess, with some strands close to becoming locs, others sticking straight, and still others as wavy as the sea.

Her hair reached past her waist, yet it was so out of order, some strands were longer than others. Her lips were the color of warm coral, and her eyelashes were so long, I couldn't stop staring.

She's a mermaid, I told myself again.

"I'm actually quite glad you can talk," she said, then looked directly at me again. "Would you be so kind as to tell me where I am?"

"You're in Kaiora Kingdom, in the Emerald forest."

"Kaiora?" She pursed her lips, as if thinking. "I've never heard of it."

"How did you get here?" I asked, and she shivered.

"I'm wondering the same thing, little..." She raised an eyebrow. "What are you, exactly? An enchanted talking frog?"

"Sort of... I'm a frog. A coqui frog." I sighed. Would she believe me if I told her I was a prince? She seemed just as lost and in need of help as I did.

"I'm a mermaid," she said, and I laughed, despite myself.

"I caught that."

She laughed too, and just the sound of it seemed to make the entire pond lighten up, as if the ripples were listening, and the leaves leaned a little towards her. I was not ignorant... there was something about her that brought life here. I'd been here long enough to tell.

"Do you know whether these ponds connect to the sea?" she asked.

"There's no ocean for miles."

"Miles?" She gaped and looked around, bewildered. "This is bad," she whispered and began pacing in the water, speaking to herself. "What happened?" she asked over and over again.

"Do you need to get to the ocean?" I asked.

She stopped and nodded. "Yes, I can't survive in fresh-water for long. I'm a mermaid. I need saltwater. I do have this potion that'll turn me into a human, but I can't take it right now because then I won't be able to talk and if I can't talk, how can I get help? And what about clothes?" She was speaking so fast, I could tell the mermaid was in a panic. The blue vial in her hand glowed.

"Whoa, slow down," I said gently, and she let out a breath.

"My father is going to *kill* me." She pulled herself on the rock and burst into tears. I gaped. This woman was over-flowing with emotions.

"Hey, hey." I said, climbing down and joining her on the rock. "It's going to be alright. We'll figure this out."

She sniffed and held out her palm so I could step onto it. Redness rimmed her beautiful eyes, but she managed another soft smile. "You're right. Something happened when I was running away from my father. I think... perhaps... magic? I rarely sense magic, but I felt it then. Maybe a portal or something opened, and I ended up here."

"What kingdom are you from?"

"The Coral Realms–it's an underwater kingdom. But the human kingdom nearby is Atlantica."

I shook my head. "That doesn't sound familiar. This is the world of the Eight Seas. There are many kingdoms here, but that's not one of them."

She let out a sigh and wiped her eyes. "Alright, so let's just assume I'm very far from home."

"And the ocean," I said.

She nodded. "Do you know the way to the ocean, little coqui?"

"My name's Ezra. Ezra Keoki."

"A pleasure to meet you." She tipped her head. "I'm Aulani."

Aulani. It had a ring to it that made me feel like I was in the ocean itself.

"Nice to meet you." A coqui chirp escaped and I sighed. "Sorry about that."

"No need to apologize." She placed me on her lap and looked around. "Do you happen to know anyone who can help me get out of here? I can't survive in freshwater for long... I need salt. I can survive maybe... a day, at most?"

For whatever reason, I feared for her. "Well, I would be more helpful if I were human," I said, and she laughed, not understanding I was very serious.

"Yes, that would probably be helpful." She hugged herself again and shivered. "I suppose being stuck here is better than my father trapping me under the water."

"He'd trap you under the water?" That sounded horrible.

"He's kind of the king of the sea," she muttered.

Wait. I blinked. Could it be...

I have to try. It was worth a shot.

"If your father is king, you're a..."

"Princess? Yes." Aulani moved her wet hair from her face. "Princess Aulani Laniakea of the Coral Realms, keeper of the royal gardens–when I'm not exploring. Oh, and recently betrothed to the barnacle-infested king of the brine."

"Congratulations?"

"Thank you. I was so overly joyful and ecstatic to spend my life in the deepest part of the ocean sweeping up whale bones and kissing the face of a crabby old man."

I visibly cringed.

"I got a potion from my aunt to become human–which of course all magic has prices to be paid..." At that, she showed me a little vial of blue potion in her hand. "I will lose my voice, and if I don't get the human prince to fall in love with me, I'll lose my voice forever, as well as turn to sea foam in a month's time."

Silence. What was I to say to that? Her situation seemed incredibly dire, with twisted options at every end.

"I might be able to help," I said.

"You're truly so sweet, but I'm not sure a frog of your size might do much. Although you have quite a loud croak."

"I'm actually a prince," I said. "Sovereign Crown Prince Ezra Keoki Kanahele of Kaiora Kingdom." She said her full title. Might as well let her know mine.

At that, she gave me a look, then smiled. "Oh, I see. You're a prince in your... frog world?"

"No, no." Why was this so frustrating to explain? "I'm a prince in the human world. I was cursed into this form... I don't know how long ago it was, but I need to get back."

Aulani looked confused, but she also seemed like she might believe anything, especially after magically transporting from her world to mine.

I quickly explained. "I was walking through the garden with the princess of Windmere when she showed me this golden ball. I think it was magic, but... I'm not sure, because we don't use magic in Kaiora. Anyway, I think it transformed me into a frog. It said any spell can be broken with the kiss from a true princess."

Aulani didn't believe me, but she looked sympathetic all the same, like she believed me to be a crazy little frog that talked.

I had to try harder. "If you kiss me and I transform back into a human, I'll help you get to the ocean. You'll probably have to turn into a human in order to survive, unless mermaids can survive out of water for a long period of time. It might take at least two days to get to the sea."

"Two days?"

"From here? Yes. We're in the deepest mountains of the island. I'm not even sure which village might be closest at this point."

"Hmm... Well, I can't survive out of water for longer than a day." She sighed and rubbed her forehead. After a moment, she added. "I've done more ridiculous things in my life. If I kiss you, and you turn back into a human, you *promise* to help me?"

"I promise. I'll do everything I can to get you to the ocean as quickly as possible."

She slipped into the water and shivered. "If you're lying and just want a kiss from a mermaid princess, I will be very vexed with you, little frog prince."

"Trust me, I'll be vexed too," I said, then closed my eyes as she leaned in to kiss me. She closed her eyes too, probably not wanting to watch herself kiss the tiny, smelly frog.

I was so small, her lips basically covered my whole head. But she smelled like coconuts and vanilla, and hot summer days. If that was all I got out of this, I'd be alright with that, especially after dealing with the feeling of being wet *all* the time. Sticky. Musty. Humid.

But Aulani? She was literally a breath of fresh air.

And suddenly she was not so big. My legs stretched out, the webbing between my fingers disappeared. The pond, which had seemed so large, now appeared small and shallow. The trees I once climbed seemed like minor branches.

For a brief moment, I was disoriented. My body ached, and my neck and back felt as if they'd been hunched over for too long. My fingers and toes stretched out, a sensation that was overwhelming since they'd been connected by webbing for so long. And the view.

I can see! I could see so much better, my vision no longer bubbled, no longer confined to my small size.

And Aulani... I could really see her.

Her eyes were closed and our faces were so close, I was tempted to kiss her just to kiss her. It was not like me to be ungentlemanlike, but I couldn't help it. What would it be like to kiss a mermaid? I leaned in and kissed her, my heart racing. This was the best first thing to do as a human.

She gasped and opened her eyes, but, much to my surprise, she didn't pull back. Instead, she wove her fingers into my hair, kissed me back, and then pulled away.

"You enjoyed yourself a little too much, frog prince." She smiled, but then her expression wavered as she took me in. Self-consciousness flooded into me, and I looked down to see that I wore the same clothes I'd been wearing when I walked through the garden with Cressida.

My shoes were gone, as I'd taken them off before stepping into the pond and transforming into a frog.

"You're..." She blinked. "You're human. You really are..."

"And I promised I'd help you," I said, regaining my composure after that kiss. Why did she kiss me back? Shouldn't she have pushed me away, or was she playing with me? She seemed like the flirty type.

Not my type, I thought. Besides, I signed betrothal papers to Cressida, a thought that filled me with dread.

"Your eyes," she said, reaching a hand to touch my face but pulling it back before we touched. "They remind me of someone."

I tipped my head.

Aulani cleared her throat. "A woman who helped me. Her eyes were a very distinct emerald color, but... probably just a coincidence."

Probably.

I stood and stretched. I'd never been so grateful to have my body back. It hurt so badly, but I also wanted to run for miles, never to hop around again.

And now I have work to do.

"Listen," I said. "If my calculations are correct, there could be a village not far from here. My cousin lives there. I could carry you there, but it might be faster if you walk. My cousin plays around with potions, and maybe she has something that could allow us to communicate, even if you do become mute when you turn into a human."

At this, Aulani bit her lower lip. She didn't want to be left alone, and I didn't blame her.

"I won't be long," I said, then smiled, which seemed to put her at ease. "I promise."

"Well." She smiled back. "You have kept your promises so far." Before I could leave though, she reached for my hand. "But... don't be gone too long, please?"

I squeezed her hand back, something electric in the air between us, something shining brighter than the sun at noon. "I'll be back soon."

CHAPTER SIX
AULANI

He wasn't what I had pictured when I imagined a frog turning into a human prince. Ezra Kanahele looked like the island had shaped him: sun-brown skin kissed countless times in the heat, salt-flecked curls falling into his eyes like he'd just come from a long swim (which he did). His hair held the faintest hint of gold, like it had stolen light from the tips of the waves themselves. And those eyes... a brighter green than even the brightest green kelp at sea.

He wasn't flashy, not even in his princely attire, but there was something quietly noble in the way he carried himself. There was a stillness, like a mountain rising from the ocean floor, steady and unshaken even when the surface was wild.

His voice was calm and genuine, cutting through any falsehood like a coral shard, and when he smiled–which was rare, crooked, a little reluctant–it felt like catching sunlight through the tides.

And that kiss? I smiled as I waited for him, trying to trust that he would come back. Hours had passed, and I was *freezing*. The dense water dried out my skin and scales, and I couldn't breathe for long underwater. Not like I wanted to go under anyway. It was too cold.

This is what life in the deep brine would be like, and I shuddered.

I made the right decision, I thought. Right? Even though I was stuck here, it was better than being trapped underwater by my father.

After a while, I began to pace. The sun had long disappeared and the moon shone in the sky.

What if he doesn't come back? What if he lied? He knew I was vulnerable out here.

He knows too much... But what choice did I have? I *had* to trust him.

As more time elapsed, I grew angry at myself. Why had I kissed him? He was the *wrong* prince to kiss! I was supposed to kiss Prince Ryker! And Prince Ryker was *realms* away.

Just as my anxiety began turning into panic, I calmed myself by singing. I could sense the life of the world around me. This island was truly something. It wasn't full of magic, but it was full of natural, innocent, unassuming life. Joyful life. Bright life. Lush life.

The trees were old, the water pure, and the leaves bent to the will of the wind. The birds occasionally sang, but they seemed... sad. Like they had lost something.

They had lost themselves. I couldn't explain how I knew this, but all mermaids had some connection to the natural world. I seemed to have this sense stronger than any other mermaid. Just as I could connect with the whales or the dolphins, I could connect with the creatures here. Which is why it surprised me when the little frog talked.

Turns out he was actually human! I looked towards the

path, and when I didn't see him, I began to sing the song I sang to Ryker after rescuing him.

E hiamoe, e hiamoe,
The tide has found you, soft and slow.
The stars above still know your name,
Even when you've lost your way.

E ho'omālie, no need to fear,
The sea carries you home from here.
I'll sing 'til breath returns to stay,
And all your sorrow drifts away.

The birds sang back, and the area, though cold and filled with mist and crisp mountain air, seemed to turn warm. A few birds descended from the trees to fly around me, as if welcoming me here. It made me feel a little less lonely.

One bird, in particular, rested on my shoulder. It seemed weak. Hungry. He looked at me with his black eyes and I paused to stroke his vibrant red head. His curved black beak tapped my skin.

"What's your name?" I asked.

It tapped me again.

"Pili?"

The bird moved its head up and down. "A pleasure to meet you." I grinned and began singing again, hoping the song would give life to the bird. The plants and water hummed in response and soon, the bird flew in circles above me.

It was just the energy it needed to find food.

"Aulani?"

I jumped, and the birds scattered away. Ezra had come

up without me even realizing it. "Were you talking to those birds?" he asked.

"Sort of." I tucked a piece of hair behind my ear and felt my heart skip a beat as he knelt down at the pool's edge to speak to me.

"Really? Can mermaids communicate with birds?"

"Not perfectly," I said. "And not all mermaids can, but... I've always had a way with animals." I held out a finger and Pili perched on it. Ezra watched, fascinated.

"This is Pili," I said. It bowed to the prince, and he grinned.

"Incredible."

"This one was hungry and weak, but a good song cheered him up and look." I tapped his head. "He found a bug to eat. Good for you."

"That is an *'apapane*," said Ezra. "One of our native songbirds." He sighed. "They're disappearing."

"Oh no." I frowned. "Why?" Then I hugged my arms as Pili flew away.

Ezra held up a vial of something green. "I'll tell you everything about the frogs on the way. My cousin has a solution for us, and it should work. The village is farther than I expected from here, but Kalei is expecting us and we're going to get you warmed up in a safe place for the night."

"Thank you." My heart warmed just from hearing his words and knowing he really kept his promise.

"Alright, so you better get your legs first," he said, "And then we'll both take this." He held up the green potion. "This will allow us to communicate, even after you lose your voice."

As I pulled out the blue vial, I hesitated.

"Is something wrong?" Ezra asked patiently.

"I'm nervous." I frowned. "I've been wanting to explore the human world for *so* long..."

"Well, you can wait a little longer and shiver, or..."

I looked up and realized... he was teasing. His eyes sparkled in the moonlight and I laughed. "You really *krilled* the mood, Ezra."

His smile made my heart flip. I thought the pun would annoy him, but he came back with a quick reply. "Careful, or I might think you're fishing for attention."

I giggled and then I didn't feel so nervous anymore as I drank the potion. It tasted awful, but as soon as I swallowed, I knew something was happening. Bright lights swirled around my body, and suddenly I could feel water rushing between my legs.

Legs! I gasped and poked my foot out of the water. I said Ezra's name, then gasped again and looked at him. My voice... it was truly gone!

"Let's get you out of the water," Ezra said, gently putting his hands under my arms to pull me out. And when he did, we both seemed to have the realization that I was, well, naked.

"Oh." Ezra quickly looked away, practically ripping off his vest and handing it to me, averting his eyes. "I honestly didn't think that through. I'm so sorry."

It's alright. Barnacles and slimy eels, he couldn't hear me! I pointed to his potion, and he nodded. "Yes, let's both drink it. Kalei said that couples use this. It works for a month at a time, which will be perfect for us. We can communicate in our minds, but the only way for it to be activated is if we..." Color blossomed in his cheeks and he rubbed the back of his neck.

I shrugged and he finished. "Is if we kiss each other."

I gave him a look.

"I promise I'm not making it up! You can even ask Kalei when we get to her house. It's like I said... couples use it when they want to communicate with their minds."

I nodded. What other choice did I have? And was it terrible I didn't mind the idea of kissing him again?

Fine. He drank half, then I drank half. It tasted much better than the one I'd just swallowed.

Then I faced Ezra and, for the first time in my whole life, my heart was racing faster than a marlin zipping away from a fisherman. My thoughts crashed like waves, relentless and wild.

His lips met mine like the hush of a tide slipping onto shore. Gentle at first, like he wasn't sure if I'd pull away. I didn't. I leaned in like a current drawn to moonlight, letting the warmth of him ripple through me, soft and sure.

Kissing Ezra was like diving into sunlit water: startling and golden, and a little dangerous if I stayed too long. I shouldn't have. I knew I shouldn't have. But oh, he tasted like the wind before a storm. I gently touched his smooth jaw, mesmerized by him. Like something I'd chased across oceans.

My heart flapped in my chest like a startled fish, flipping wildly between *you fool, stop kissing him!* and *do it again!* His fingers brushed the back of my neck, and I swear the sea inside me sang.

This wasn't just a kiss. It was a *breach*—the kind whales make when they can't help but leap into the sky.

And *tides take it!* I wanted to leap with him.

I shouldn't have enjoyed it as much as I did, but he didn't pull away, so why should I?

This is a shipwreck and I'm sinking for it.

Ezra's voice sounded as he pulled away. *Really? Good to know.*

My embarrassment could've drowned a whole reef.

You heard that?

I can hear everything. You can probably hear my thoughts too, though I'm trying to keep them guarded. And suddenly I felt our connection. I *could* see his thoughts, but as he said, he raised walls, made out of tall, sturdy trees, to block me from the view of him. I did get a glimpse of the words and emotions he felt: attraction, guilt, and... admiration?

If he asks to kiss me again, I don't think I could say no.

I heard that too. He spoke to me in my mind again and grinned.

Well, this is going swimmingly. By which I mean I'm sinking fast. I had to build up a wall in my mind, like his.

Coral. Yes. I was from the Coral Realms and we used coral as walls for everything. I built it up, keeping him out of my intrusive and wild thoughts.

Ezra's green eyes sparkled in the moonlight. *You wear your heart on your sleeve, mermaid.*

If I had one, I teased and he smiled, standing and helping me up.

"Let's get you to the ocean," he said. As I took his hands, I felt as if my entire world was shifting.

Shifting... But how? I was probably delirious from being in this new world.

It most certainly was *not* Ezra.

With his tunic around my waist, I attempted to stand. Ezra's calloused hands settled on my waist, but then he quickly retracted them, as if burned. His face flushed.

"You're... steady now?"

Not in the slightest. How do you stand so straight on these wobbly things? They're worse than seaweed.

It was then I could tell he kept looking away, averting his eyes.

Ah. I gently lifted his chin so he met my eyes. *You have no idea, do you? I've seen much worse. Consider this modest compared to the world I came from.*

He blinked, processing what I'd said, then the faint pink on his cheeks deepened. "I... I don't..." The silence stretched, thick and uncomfortable. What was I to do to make him more comfortable?

Then, a fleeting thought came into our shared connection, whispering between us: *She's... unbelievably attractive.*

My eyes widened and I couldn't help but smile, amused. *Oh really?*

He froze. "That's–I mean..."

Thank you, Ezra. That's good to know.

He cursed to himself and let out a breath. "Look. I didn't mean–I mean... I never said I wasn't aware of it. Just–" He sighed. "I'm not used to the company of someone like you."

No need to explain yourself, I told him. *I'm not offended.*

He let out another breath and I couldn't tell if he was relieved or more embarrassed than before... but something about the interaction made my heart skip a beat. I'd been called beautiful before, but, coming from him... it was different. It made my heart want to soar and sail wild and free like the ships on the sea.

I'm not so different from the company you probably keep, Ezra. I'm just... more exposed.

And this time Ezra let out a nervous laugh as he rubbed the back of his neck.

"Right. Um... we'll see. So let's teach you how to walk and get you some real clothes." And with that, he placed his hands on my waist to steady me. I took his arms, and, in a few electric moments, my jellyfish legs steadied enough for me to walk on my own.

Just a few steps.

More stumbles that frustrated me more than I wanted to admit.

But I got the hang of it. Mostly.

"You did it!" he exclaimed, leaned over, his hands still on my waist. I clapped my hands, but, for some reason, he was still there, and I didn't want him to let go. We looked into each other's eyes, and my heart paddled harder than a panicked seahorse.

Oh scales. We had to get me to my world, because if I spent too much time with this young man, I was going to sink farther than the briney kingdom at the bottom of the sea.

CHAPTER SEVEN
EZRA

Even I had to admit that kissing a mermaid was probably the most exhilarating thing I'd ever done in my life. It was strange to think that when I was last human, Princess Cressida might have wanted to kiss me. And that filled my stomach with dread.

I knew I shouldn't think it, especially because Aulani had her own world and prince to return to, probably oceans away, but I secretly wondered what it would be like if she stayed. Was it *absolutely* necessary that I marry the woman who was once betrothed to my brother? My father said I was taking Tavo's place, but did that include taking the woman he was meant to wed? Did I really have to follow the guidance and advice of my father and the counselors?

Aulani grabbing my arm swiftly distracted me from my roiling stomach. Her big brown eyes sparkled in the moonlight as she smiled up at me. *Sorry I keep grabbing you like a drunk sailor on a steady ship*, she said to my mind. *Just when I think I get the hang of these legs, they keep swaying like kelp on a bad day.*

The corner of my lip turned up. Every part of Aulani was

bubbling and overflowing with joy. It was becoming increasingly difficult to keep my composure around her. I had given her my shirt a while back, which made me feel much too exposed with a naked upper body, but she didn't seem to mind. She even said that mermen never wore shirts or clothes, so it didn't bother her.

It bothered me though. What was the mermaid's life really like? Did she have a lover back in her kingdom? Or was she in love with that human prince she mentioned?

I shouldn't care. So why did it nag at me?

On our walk through the forest, I told her everything that had happened to me: taking my brother's place, the walk in the garden with Cressida, the fight against the invasive frogs, and trying to help the songbirds thrive again.

You've got a lot on your shoulders Ezra, she said after I finished. *Honestly, I can see why you're so stressed now.*

Stressed?

She laughed. *Yes. Ever since I met you, you're tight and serious as a hungry stingray.*

I glanced at her and she squeezed my arm. *You'll get it all sorted, Ezra. I know you will.*

Her confidence in me was encouraging, especially when she didn't even know me. I smiled to myself, but hoped she didn't realize the effect she was having on me... especially in such a short span of time.

When we reached the village, I spoke softly. "It's probably best if people don't see us..."

Especially like this? She grinned and looked me up and down. I became self conscious of my frame. I was never as big and bulky like Tavo, but I did try to take care of myself, and I knew I had a strong, toned physique. My muscles still ached, something I hoped would go away as I stayed human for a while.

But, for some reason, I hoped she found me agreeable. From the light humming coming from her mind to mine, I figured I was agreeable to her.

I nodded. *Yes. We can't let anyone see us... Especially not like this. It'll be the scandal of all time and I do not need more marks against me.*

What do you mean? She clutched my arm as we wove through the empty streets, ducking into alleys and under windows. I liked the way she held me, her hands warm and smooth like coconut milk. But she really did walk like a drunk person.

I would never tell her that, of course. She'd been a mermaid her whole life, and, considering how long she'd been a human, she was doing pretty good.

My older brother was supposed to rule, but he died in foreign lands months ago, I said. *I've since taken his place and it's been... rough.*

Oh I'm so sorry Ezra, she said, and the compassion in her voice nearly melted me. She really did wear her heart on her sleeve.

I'm expected to wed Princess Cressida of Windmere. We were going to discuss the betrothal on our walk through the gardens. I had just signed the papers that morning before meeting with her.

Aulani wrinkled her nose. *That barnacle of a princess who abandoned you in the pool? Oh I'd have a word with her if I could talk!*

I chuckled. *Maybe you shouldn't be calling people names, especially when you haven't met them yet.*

She deserves it for what she did to you. You said she looked right at you! How could she not *know you were transformed into a frog? Was she blind?*

No.

Exactly my point. Aulani's grip tightened on my arm, as if to emphasize her thoughts. *I've never met her, but I don't trust her.*

Our conversation was cut short.

"We're here," I said. I gently knocked on the door, looking around to make sure the streets were still empty. The homes here were plantation homes: boxy, simple structures made out of wood, jalousie windows, and tin roofs. Raindrops softly drummed the roof as a light rain began.

Come on, Kalei... Just when I started worrying that Kalei wasn't home, the door opened. My cousin stood there, as short as the mermaid princess beside me. Her dark, wavy hair was pulled back into a loose bun and her dark eyes narrowed as she took us in.

I could sense her burning questions, but she relaxed and smiled. "Hurry, come inside. Both of you." And with that, she shut the door behind us. Kalei rushed to close the curtains. Someone was already in the small living space, and when he stood, he was as tall as myself.

Relief flooded me. "Hoʻohuli." We hugged and he seemed to hold me extra tight.

"We all thought you were dead," he said. This man was my father's first counselor and my own mentor. Sometimes Sir Anani Hoʻohuli felt more like a father to me than my own father.

"There's so much to tell you," he said.

"But first let's get them bathed and properly dressed," Kalei said, holding a bundle of towels in her hands. "She smells like the sea and you smell like a musty old frog."

Aulani laughed at that and Kalei smiled at her. "I'm

Kalei Kanahele," she said, holding out her hand, adding, "Ezra's crazy cousin."

"You're not crazy."

"You hesitated." Kalei's eyes narrowed at me.

Aulani laughed again, though she was mute as ever, and it hurt my heart that they wouldn't get to hear her beautiful voice.

At least I *get to hear her voice.*

I heard that. The mermaid princess glanced at me and smiled, which made my heart race faster than a rushing waterfall.

"Hoʻohuli brought some clothes for you, Ezra. You can bathe outside in the back and I'll help Aulani in my own washroom."

Are you going to be alright? I asked and Aulani nodded enthusiastically.

I like your cousin already, Ezra!

Just call me if you need anything.

Her expression softened. *You too.*

So she went with Kalei while I went out back, using a bucket to dump cold freshwater on myself from Kalei's catchment tank. Rain gutters from the rooftop went into this large catchment tank made of lava rock and cement.

The sound of coqui frogs broke the silence, and I glared into the dark forest behind her home.

Wretched frogs. I wished it was the sound of birds I heard, not the invasive species.

When I finished, I stepped into the house, towel wrapped around my waist.

"Here you are," Hoʻohuli said, handing me the clothes and I changed in the kitchen. I caught a glimpse of my reflection in the jalousie window and insecurity passed through me.

How much time had passed since I'd been a frog? Was father going to be disappointed with me?

It doesn't matter, I told myself. The main thing right now was that Aulani had to get back to the sea, so she could find her kingdom again and get home.

So she can marry Prince Ryker. Ryker? I didn't even like the sound of his name. I helped myself to the food Kalei brought out, most likely for us. The soft bread with lilikoi jam never tasted so good, and the kalua pig and rice was the most satisfying thing I'd ever eaten in my life.

I massaged the back of my neck as I closed my eyes, savoring the taste of real food.

Not bugs.

And then relief panged my heart. I was fine. I no longer had to keep checking my surroundings. There was no longer a need to constantly be on the lookout for frog catchers, or other bigger frogs.

No more survival.

I was safe here in Kalei's home.

It was disorienting, and I jumped when I heard her voice.

"Missed real food?" Kalei stepped into the kitchen and began placing everything onto trays to take to the dining space.

"Yes... a lot. This is delicious, Kalei. Thanks for having us... on such late notice and at this hour–"

"Keoki." She always called me by my island name. "You know I'd do anything for you." Kalei paused in her work and put her hands on my arms, water pooling in her eyes. "I'm just *so* glad you're alive." Then we hugged. That was when Aulani walked in.

Excuse me... She quickly turned around, probably feeling awkward at interrupting us. I sensed a fleeting flash of jealousy rip through her coral walls but she grabbed it back and smiled.

Can I help?

"Sure." I handed her a tray and then paused.

You look... She was all dressed now, with a white wrap around blouse, the long sleeves loose and hanging effortlessly. Wrapped around her waist was a flowing blue skirt, which only accentuated her petite frame.

Human? She grinned.

Beautiful.

Aulani's eyes sparkled. *Thank you, Ezra. And you clean up nicely too.* Then she skipped off to the dining room, where Hoʻohuli showed her how to set the table.

"Oof." Kalei looked from the mermaid to me. "I can't even *hear* what you guys are saying to each other in your minds, but whatever is going on between you is making this room warm."

"Kalei!"

She giggled and nudged me, stepping into the dining room. We were all famished, and Aulani endlessly complimented the food. *This tastes so good!* She overflowed with excitement as she tried everything. Her expressions were exaggerated, but it was so... *her.* She'd close her eyes as she tasted the lilikoi jam, then thoughtfully eat the pork, saying she was not accustomed to eating animals but it was something she could get used to as long as she was grateful.

When her excitement died down and I didn't have to say aloud to Kalei and Hoʻohuli what the mermaid was thinking, we settled in the living space and spoke.

"So how have things been?" I asked, and Kalei and Hoʻohuli exchanged nervous looks. I had been a little suspicious of them wanting to keep me hidden, especially when I first arrived at Kalei's house for the potion. She looked like she had seen a ghost.

And, now, her face paled.

"Is something wrong?" I asked.

Hoʻohuli leaned forward, resting his elbows on his knees. He was an older man, with graying hair and wrinkles on the corners of his eyes. I trusted him with my life, as my father had done.

"Why didn't you send for my father?" I asked Kalei. When she said she'd go to the palace, I thought she'd noise abroad that I was back. But it seemed all of this had been done in secret. And the fact that she'd closed the windows and the curtains meant... something was off.

Hoʻohuli nodded to her. "He should hear it from you."

"Keoki." She began wringing her hands. "You've been gone for almost a year."

"Months," I said, hoping to correct her. She shook her head.

"But... I just turned into a frog a few days ago... I couldn't have been gone that long..." The world started spinning.

"Your father... Uncle Kimo..." Kalei pursed her lips and looked down, water pooling in her eyes again.

Oh no. I could sense what she said before the words left her lips.

"He looked everywhere for you. The princess said that you just disappeared in the garden, and everyone in the kingdom has been terrified that there's magic here... something we're not used to, something that's foreign to us..."

"But where's my father?"

"He searched the entire island for you, and when he couldn't find you, he left to get help from other kingdoms. And on his way back..."

Aulani sat forward, her eyes wide.

A tear fell down Kalei's cheek. "The ship encountered a storm and your father didn't survive."

My father... lost. Gone. All air was sucked out of me. I stood and Aulani stood too.

"I didn't want to tell you until I knew you were safe. But you need to know. Keoki, Uncle Kimo, your father is gone. Princess Cressida has taken over. She says no one can leave the kingdom. No one goes to the sea. Not anymore."

Ho'ohuli nodded. "It's been a dictatorship."

I stared at my hands, too stunned to speak, my fingers curling into fists.

Ezra... Aulani's voice was gentle.

"I'm sorry I didn't tell you sooner," Kalei said. "But the palace is sealed like a fortress. People are scared. Some of the nobles have sided with her. Others are vanishing."

Aulani's breath caught and she put her hands over her mouth, shocked.

"I should've been there," I said, rage building within me. "I should've been there. None of this would've happened–my father, Cressida–if I had just *been there.*"

"It's not your fault," Ho'ohuli said. "Someone cursed you and–"

Cressida cursed you, Aulani cut in though the others couldn't hear her.

"We can't assume it was her," I said aloud and Ho'ohuli agreed, though he hadn't heard Aulani's thought. He knew what she assumed.

"It could have been anyone hidden in the garden that day."

"How long ago did my father die?" I asked.

"A month or two after you disappeared," Kalei answered. "The whole kingdom mourned for days, Keoki...

both for you and for your father. It's like a cloud has hung over Kaiora since you've both been gone. And with Lady Cressida on the throne, we're all terrified. She's brought in her own armies and powers, and nobody can get to the sea. Nobody can get out, while foreigners can come in."

I'm so sorry Ezra. Aulani gently stroked my arm, and her touch seemed to calm something inside of me. But the calm was quickly replaced by anger.

More anger. *Cressida took over my kingdom...* And all because I signed those betrothal papers.

You have to take back the throne, Aulani said.

"No, I have to get you to the ocean before it's too late."

She shook her head. *Listen to yourself. Your father is gone. Your kingdom needs you. You need time to grieve and–*

I turned to her, my voice raw with grief and anger. "I'll grieve later. If you don't get back to the ocean, you'll die."

Silence. All eyes watched Aulani as she stepped closer and gently took my hand. *I care more about you than the sea right now.*

I couldn't help but catch her hand and press it to my cheek. My emotions were a storm right now, and she was the calm. I was terrified, angry, and alone... yet I wasn't.

"Well, I care more about you living. We'll figure everything else out after that."

Kalei and Hoʻohuli stood there, my mentor averting his eyes while Kalei watched with fascination. "You two are a mess," she said, breaking the tension and I quickly let go of Aulani's hand. She stepped away from me too. "But you're perfect."

"Kalei–"

She smiled, but there were tears in her eyes. "Whatever Aulani said, she's right. You're not getting anywhere until you're ruler of Kaiora Kingdom again."

"But you can't just barge in," Ho'ohuli said. "We must be strategic."

"We've already discussed the plans," Kalei added. "Cressida is holding a masquerade ball and has invited the nobles from the kingdom, including myself, surprisingly. I think word has reached her ears that I do happen to know a little something about potion-making."

My eyes narrowed. What was Kalei getting at?

"You're going to go as my companion," she said, then turned to Aulani. "And you can go as me. I'm sure you'll enjoy the ball more than I do anyways. I hate those sorts of things. Keoki knows. When you're there, you can see how things are and have a grand reveal in front of everyone. There's nothing she'll be able to do about it!"

Aulani's expression lightened up, but then she turned to me. *What do you say, Ezra?*

I promise *I'll take you to the sea, Aulani, as soon as we take the throne.*

She winked, then nudged my arm. *If not, I do hear foamy oblivion is lovely this time of year.*

Aulani... The corner of my lip twitched anyway.

She squeezed my hand. *I know Ezra. You keep your promises, don't you?*

I squeezed her hand back. I shouldn't have, but I did. She had to know I was going to do this... all of this, not just for myself, my kingdom, Kalei, or Ho'ohuli... but for her. I wasn't going to let her month pass up and she turned to sea foam. I'd help her return to her realm, no matter the cost. I owed her my life, after all. *Yes, I do. Always.*

CHAPTER EIGHT
AULANI

I lied awake on the settee, nestled in bundles of blankets, while Ezra slept on the ground. Ho'ohuli left earlier that night and Kalei slept in her room. I listened to the prince's soft and steady breathing, relishing every moment that day. So much had happened in such a short space of time, and I was exhausted.

Not too exhausted to think about my electric relationship with Ezra though. He was a perfect prince: kind, noble, gentle.

Gentle. I adored that about him. The way he spoke to me, the way his eyes sparkled when I made him laugh... I found myself smiling in the darkness, daydreaming of a future I knew could not be.

Get yourself together Aulani. You're like a confused shrimp getting swallowed by a whale. Not only must you return to your realm, but you just met him. Right. I was supposed to get Prince Ryker to fall in love with and marry me, not Ezra.

And, right. What girl daydreamed about a life with a man she just met? That was the stuff of fairy tales, not my story. Ezra was distracting me from my mission, which was to win the heart of the right prince: Prince Ryker.

As soon as we get Ezra's throne back, he'll take me to the sea. And once we reached the sea, I'd be able to tell if it connected to my sea, a thought that filled me with dread and excitement.

I have to get back. Every second I spent here was another second *not* in my realm. A second closer to turning into sea foam.

As I drifted off to sleep, I heard Ezra stir. He slipped out of his makeshift bed and stepped into the back of the house. I didn't immediately move.

Where is he going? Curiosity got the best of me. I stepped out the back door, finding him standing at the edge of the forest, his back towards me, his hands clasped behind him.

He stared into the darkness.

It suddenly occurred to me that he probably wanted to be alone. He had just found out his father died. A dictator ruled over his kingdom. He had to reclaim the throne. And, to add to all of it, he took it upon himself to take me to the sea as soon as possible.

Not to mention he was finally a human after a year of being in survival mode as a pesky frog. He probably needed a moment of peace away from everyone and everything, including me.

Just as I turned, Ezra's voice gently spoke to me. *Stay.*

I hesitated, but he spoke again. *I find your presence calming, Aulani.* Then he turned and beckoned for me to join him at the edge of the forest. I did so, my heart pattering at his confession. My bare feet sank into the soft, dewy grass.

He finds my presence calming? Why did that make me want to dance in delight? I stood close to him so our arms touched, and he didn't move away. He glanced at me, then continued to look into the darkness, the coqui frogs chirping beyond.

After a long moment, I gently touched Ezra's arm. *Are you alright?*

He looked at my hand and I quickly withdrew it, self-conscious of any touch between us. It was then I realized a tear slipped down Ezra's cheek. My heart stopped, or it felt like it.

He's grieving. This man, who barely let his emotions show, was now having a moment. And he was allowing me to be a part of it. I don't know why, but I never felt more connected. I had not lost my parents, but I could only imagine how difficult that would be.

Yet, I would lose my parents, if I already hadn't been disowned by them. That caused my own heart to seize up. I still had parents, but his were gone. Completely gone.

I thought I'd have more time, he said, his voice rough. *Just a little more. A chance to prove I wasn't a failure.*

I stepped closer. *You weren't–you're not, Ezra.*

His eyes burned... not with anger, but a desperate, deep kind of ache that not even the tides could read. *He probably died thinking I abandoned the island, our kingdom, our people.*

I hesitated, then said, *You were cursed, Ezra. None of that was your fault.*

His breach hitched. Our eyes met. And that was when something inside of him broke loose. His shoulders buckled, a sound catching in his throat as another tear fell. He turned away fast, but I didn't let him retreat.

I shouldn't... I don't... His words were jumbled and confused. Crumbling, even, like dried coral being crushed under waves, turning into rocky sand. His legs gave just a little, and he sank to one knee, then both. Not collapsing, exactly... just surrendering.

I dropped with him, folding my arms around his shoulders, pressing his face gently against my collarbone as his grief poured out like freshwater into the sea. He didn't sob. Ezra wasn't the kind of man who was loud. But his body trembled, his breathing sharp and uneven.

I cradled his head, one hand sliding into his hair, the other arm holding him steady.

You're not alone, Ezra, I said softly, sensing his deep feelings, ones that he was trying to keep hidden. But no matter how hard he tried, I could feel it there. Loneliness. Aching, dark, deep loneliness. His brother was gone. His father was gone.

And, as if reading my own thoughts, he said softly, *My mother disappeared when I was young... I barely remember her.*

How alone he must have felt in this world! His mother lost at a young age, growing up in the shadow of his brother, only to lose him and become heir to the throne... all while trying to prove something to his father. It made me love him even more.

Love? I closed my eyes. Yes. It wasn't a romantic love, but genuine compassion. I wished I could do more for him, help him more. But this was all I could do right now.

We stayed like that for a long time: two souls at the edge of the dark forest, under a cacophonic medley of coqui frog chirps. A prince with no throne. A mermaid with no sea. And something soft and fragile blooming between.

"YOU LOOK STUNNING!" Kalei turned me around and around in front of the mirror. "Yes, yes. As long as you keep your hair covered like that, you could pass for me." She had pulled my hair back into a loose bun, then fastened flowers and other tropical foliage to detract from the color of my hair, which looked nothing like Kalei's.

She handed me the mask and I put it on, rather hating the way I looked. It was not me. I wore a light blue dress with sequins that dotted the hem, making it look like sea swirls at noon. The bodice was full of even more matching sequins that dazzled in the light. The sequined mask covered my eyes and nose, with dramatic feathers coming out of the top, another smart way to cover my hair.

Ezra wore green, his outfit less sequined than mine. His green mask made his eyes stand out even more, and when we stood in front of each other, I laughed.

I feel so silly.

Trust me, what we're wearing is simple compared to what others will be wearing. He offered his arm as he led me to the carriage. After spending the day with Kalei, I discovered that she was rather wealthy… which made sense. She was the cousin of the king, and her parents were nobles. Since she was the same twenty years old as myself and not yet wed, her parents gave her a large sum of money to make her way in the world and she did. She owned her own home but also a shop down the road, where she sold natural medicines and remedies… and maybe a potion or two.

With a bubbly and snarky personality, as well as a cheerful countenance, Kalei was a joy to be around. She was still young. Why hadn't any man come and snatched her up?

"Hoʻohuli is going to meet you both there," she said, nervousness in her eyes as she went over the plans for the hundredth time.

"Ezra." She took her cousin's hand. "*Please* be careful. One wrong move and she could kill you without anyone knowing. They *must* all learn you're alive at the right moment."

"I'll be careful." Ezra said. He and Kalei kissed one another's cheeks. I had been here long enough to learn it was an island custom to kiss one another's cheeks in greeting or farewell. I'd seen Kalei and Ho'ohuli do it, so it did not alarm me.

"Enjoy yourselves," Kalei said, adding, "And make sure Ezra dances at least once. He says he doesn't know how, but he's the best dancer around." She nodded to us both. "Now go and get the kingdom back."

With that, she closed the carriage door and stepped back, waving to us. My nerves flared up like a lionfish spreading its massive fan-like fins.

So I attempted to distract myself by looking out the window at the enchanting sights. After such a late night, Ezra and I slept in longer than we probably should have, and I didn't get much of a chance to explore... although I knew there was no time for that.

Our priority was to get Ezra the throne, help me find my way back home, and *then* I could explore the human world. Well, once I got back home. But there was so much here! So many sights. Sounds. And *people!*

Do you like it?

I looked up to see Ezra watching me, and my heart skipped a beat. *Yes, very much. I don't think that it's like this in the human kingdom by my sea, but... perhaps it's similar.*

For whatever reason, a sinking feeling trickled down my throat. *What if it's not all that I hoped it to be?* I'd only been here a day, at most, but would all of this become boring? Mundane? What if there wasn't much I could learn from the humans, or study the stars as I wished?

You're allowed to let your dreams change, Ezra said, and I realized he could read my thoughts. It was as if I'd been saying it all aloud to him.

I sat back and sighed. *Yes, but I'm determined to make the human world better than the sea.*

Ezra was quiet for a moment, then said, *When I was younger, I always dreamed of becoming a master gardener and helping our land be self sustainable. I wanted to find ways to sustain the native and indigenous plants while still catering to the foreigners growing their plantations and crops.* Ezra leaned forward, his face so close I could see golden flecks in his eyes. *Then Tavo died, and I became heir to the throne. I never tucked away those dreams though... Since learning that I was to become king, I've planned ways to incorporate that into my new role.*

But I can't go back to the underwater world. It's awful...

Not all of it, right? He raised an eyebrow.

Right. I would definitely miss swimming with the dolphins, meeting the eyes of the whales, tending sea gardens, and so much more... I sighed. *I just want the human world to be everything I imagined... or else... I left my old life for nothing...*

Can't both have their ups and downs? Not everything in life is perfect.

My lip twitched. Ezra reminded me of sea turtles, always full of so much wisdom, even the young ones.

Thank you. I've been a frog before, so we'll add sea turtle to my list of amphibious natures.

I laughed. *Ezra!* I was *not* good at keeping my thoughts masked from him. Not one bit... and for whatever reason I kind of liked it.

. . .

When we reached the palace, I gaped again. "Masks on," Ezra said and I quickly obeyed. True to his word, Ho'ohuli waited for us.

"Lady Kalei Kanahele and Sir Eli Court." Sir Eli Court was the secret name Ho'ohuli made up for Ezra. The counselor kissed my cheek and hugged Ezra, then motioned for us to follow him. Instead of the grand entryway, he took us through a side door.

"Everyone is here tonight," he said quietly to Ezra. "This will be the perfect opportunity to reveal yourself. I will follow your lead." He added, "Just don't let her see you before the moment..."

My hands grew clammy as I looked around.

Chandeliers glowed like jellyfish in a dark sea, illuminating the room with their crystals sparkling in the light. Music echoed through the spacious chambers, opulent and surreal. As we entered, masked, we blended right in with the nobles.

And Ezra was right.

Compared to others, we did look quite simple. Diamonds, bows, sequins, lace, feathers, and flowers adorned every person around us. They almost did not look like humans, but human bodies with bird faces. I stood a little closer to Ezra, and, as if sensing my nervousness, he offered his arm. I took it, probably holding it tighter than what was comfortable.

As we passed people, I couldn't help but notice the way they spoke to each other, so different from the way Kalei or Ho'ohuli interacted with us. They laughed loudly, tossing their heads back. They eyed us, looking us up and down as if our attire was not worthy of their attention. Some ate and kept eating. Others danced, their conversations disappearing as they came and went around the floor.

Let's dance. Though surprised that Ezra suggested it, I joined him without hesitation. I was dying to dance, especially since I had much more confidence with my legs and feet.

My nerves eased a little as Ezra pulled me close to him, one hand on my waist, the other holding my hand. I looked up into his bright green eyes and smiled.

I like you better without all of this gaudy stuff, he said. *I mean. You're always beautiful, but you don't need all of this to enhance your appearance. The people here... they do.*

I laughed at that. *Why thank you, Ezra. Like a guppy being complimented for swimming straight.*

He smiled, and my heart raced as his words echoed in my mind: *You're always beautiful...*

I stumbled around like an octopus moving across sand, stepping on the prince's toes more than a few times. But he didn't seem to mind. His eyes scanned the room and he drew me closer, as if protecting me.

There she is.

I followed his gaze to a young woman sitting on the throne, a tight corset accentuating her curves. Her hair was so pale it almost blended into her skin. Her icy blue eyes watched, as if she were looking for something wrong.

She looks like a jellyfish. Pretty to look at, but all sting beneath the surface.

Ezra's stoic expression broke for a moment. *She's my betrothed, Aulani.*

I know, and I don't trust her. Who are all those men standing around her?

Ezra glanced again. *Some are her guards. Others are noblemen from here... I don't recognize all of them. They're probably her suitors.*

That made me want to gag. She looked around her like they were her loyal seadogs.

The song ended and another one started, one that was quicker than the last one. People around us started the new dance, causing Ezra and I to drift apart.

Aulani...

I'm alright. I stood to the side, watching as Ezra got looped into the dance. He kept searching for me, but I assured him. *I'm fine, Ezra. And you are a fine dancer.*

I did rather enjoy watching him. He moved as if he was always grounded, like every step meant something.

"Once all the troops come in, the plantation owners will arrive and things can finally get moving."

A man's voice drew my attention away from the prince. The voice was high pitched as he prattled away about something. I couldn't help but move deeper into the crowd to get closer and hear more.

What troops? Plantation owners?

"I'm looking forward to it," said another man. I could see their faces now. One man had dark hair and a mustache that curled up on the edges. The curl resembled an upside down sea horse tail. The other man had flaming red hair, something I couldn't stop staring at. Though mermaids had hair in every color, I'd never seen anyone with ginger hair. He was a big man, so big that even his mask could not fit on his face. He reminded me of a grouper fish, all jowls and bulk, as if the ocean had sculpted him out of leftover stone.

Seahorse mustache, on the other end, was completely slim. "In just a few days, she's going to ban the primitive festivals these people host. That, their pagan *hula* dancing, and worship at those barbaric sites."

They spoke as if the natives of the island were animals. I scowled, but quickly smiled and shook my head as a servant held out a tray of food, offering me to partake. He nodded and went on his way.

"Yes, she's doing a swell job of civilizing these people and their island customs," said grouper fish.

"And once the people here learn their place, the island will truly thrive."

I shuddered. *They're trying to erase the soul of the island.* It was the people who kept the island alive. Their respect for the land was evident in the way that Ezra treated it. Sure, I hadn't known him for very long, but just in the short time I *did* know him, I knew that he loved his people and his home.

"Here's a pretty face."

I blinked, suddenly realizing that seahorse mustache had noticed me standing around and approached. "May I have the next dance?" he asked.

No thank you... But my voice was gone. I frantically looked around. Where was Ezra?

"Ah, you are a shy one." He grinned. "What is your name, pretty little thing?"

Little thing? I gaped before my eyebrows furrowed. I was not a *thing!* My fists balled and the man had the audacity to take another step.

"Don't be shy. My name is Edward Lucillen, and I am one of the High Lady Cressida's counselors. You can rest assured I'm honorable."

Does he even know what honor means? I shook my head and he reached for my wrist.

"Come, just one dance."

"Don't touch her." My racing heart calmed as Ezra stepped in, placing his hand on my waist, as if claiming me as his own.

Ezra! I nodded enthusiastically to the man, but he was

staring at the prince.

"You look..."

"If a woman does not want to dance with you, Edward," he said, "I suggest you leave her alone." A circle slowly formed around us, as the man let out a scream.

"He's... alive?"

"Who is it?" someone muttered near us.

"It's him!" Another one burst in.

Ho'ohuli was there in a moment. "It's the prince!" he exclaimed loudly, his eyes sparkling because he knew it all along.

And then the music stopped as Cressida, sitting on the throne, rose, her face pale. "Ezra?"

Beside me, Ezra took off his mask and a ripple of gasps escaped around the room. "It's the prince!"

"He's alive!"

More than terror, like the look on Edward's face, was the relief in the room. It felt like a gentle wave over the water's surface, the kind that lapped on the boards of the ships, not crashed against it.

Cressida's expression mirrored that of seahorse mustache and his grouper fish friend, but then her face broke into a smile, one that showed relief and joy.

"Prince Ezra, you're alive and well!" Tears pooled in her eyes and I frowned. I suppose I expected her to give him a cold welcome, but she ran down the throne and threw her arms around him, giving him a big hug. Those in the room said soft "oohs" and "awws." She had thrown herself so forcefully on him, he didn't have a chance to move or recoil, and his hands fell from my waist.

Jealousy sucked the air from me like squid tentacles. I knew this was his betrothed–or was? And I would be leaving, but I felt a stinging hatred for her, something I'd never experienced before.

Ezra stood back awkwardly, giving them space. He hardly hugged her back, his eyebrows furrowed. "I am back," he said. "I was able to break my curse, with some help." His eyes met mine, and I nodded encouragingly. Cressida gave me a cutting look, then quickly covered it with a smile.

"But I am back," he said, then took a step away from Cressida. "And I've returned to reclaim what's mine."

I wanted to clap my hands at the whole scene. I'd never been so proud of Ezra in my life, and that was saying something when I'd known him only a day or so.

CHAPTER NINE
EZRA

I was back. The entire room silenced as every head bowed. The guards, which had surrounded Cressida, now made their way towards me.

"As heir to the throne, Ezra Keoki Kanahele is the rightful king of Kaiora Kingdom," said Ho'ohuli, stepping forward. He congratulated me with a hug, then many others followed, teary-eyed, welcoming me and wanting to know what occurred.

I tried to explain things, but Ho'ohuli helped out by saying he would send out a royal decree immediately explaining that the beloved Crown Prince of Kaiora had been turned to a frog by a curse–which would very well be investigated–but that he was back and would be crowned king.

I'm back.

The rest of the night was a whirlwind as my servants, guards, and counselors thronged me. Cressida seemed to all but fade away and Aulani stood to the side, folding her arms and watching, a big smile on her face. She looked nothing but proud of me, and that made my insides soar.

. . .

I PROMISED Aulani I'd take her to the sea as soon as I became king, but the next few days had me swamped. And not in a frog kind of way.

The political climate had escalated in my absence. Foreign ambassadors demanded attention. Wealthy businessmen and merchants were forcing natives to sell their land. Gates, to keep people away from the sea, had to be torn down. Armies needed to be dissembled and sent home. Some of my most trusted advisors and counselors had gone "missing" and I sent out immediate investigations. It was an absolute mess.

Aulani didn't seem to mind though. She stayed in the guest quarter–much too far from me, in my personal opinion–and spent the day exploring with Kalei while I attended meetings, made laws, and eagerly awaited my coronation day. I had to admit, I did wish I could join them. Anytime I looked out a window and saw the two young women walking through the gardens or exploring the palace grounds, my heart ached to be the man to show Aulani this world.

When people asked who, "Who is the girl next to the king?" My closest counselors, who knew the secret, decided on a cover up. We didn't want her or I to be the face of a scandal, so we made the decision to tell them she was an esteemed guest of the king's. She was from a foreign land and helped break my curse. Much to my relief, nobody asked any more questions about the mute girl who held my arm any time we walked to dinner, or who sometimes waited impatiently outside the throne room while I held meetings. Well, at least not to my face. I was sure gossip spread about us, but I didn't really care. Probably because I liked being with her.

And, if I was honest, it was rather... exciting that she was eager to spend time with me. I secretly wished our time together was longer.

But there's so much to do. Especially if I was going to take her to the sea.

Meanwhile, Cressida did not give me an audience. Whenever I scheduled a time to meet with her, a messenger would tell me she was sick or otherwise not feeling well.

Finally, however, she came to dinner. Ever since the big reveal, I terminated our betrothal and announced that I would rule as a sovereign king, not marrying to strengthen ties with foreign lands. I would find other ways to strengthen our ties, and I hadn't seen or heard from Cressida since.

She was in the palace, but she avoided me, and I didn't do anything to kick her out, but she had overstayed her welcome and put my kingdom through the mud.

There had to be consequences, but her supporters cried out that she was innocent.

She sat at the table, smiling prettily at everyone around her and batting her eyes at me. Tension pulled the air between us, like a taught line with a fray that threatened to unravel at any moment. She wore her tight corset and a pastel pink dress that made her fair skin appear even fairer.

Next to me, Aulani wore a flowing white blouse and sea-blue skirt that enhanced her natural features. She wore shell jewelry, big hoops with dangling sea glass hanging from her ears, and rings on her fingers made of wood, shells, and metal. I wasn't sure where she'd gotten all of it–perhaps Kalei took her to the market and they'd purchased some jewelry. When our eyes met, she smiled, and the corner of my lip turned up. Her attention turned to all the food that was served to us, her thoughts happy and bright, like light dancing through the trees. She was always so fascinated by everything, and it was hard not to get caught up in her zest for life.

"This seafood is *so* good," Princess Cressida said, drawing attention towards herself. "I imagine it's freshly caught? You do love supporting the locals, don't you Ezra?"

I swallowed a sip of chilled coconut water, giving her a cool look. "The ʻaina takes care of us when we take care of it. The locals are accustomed to taking care of the land and sea when they fish. Their nets and hooks don't cause collateral damage, unlike foreigners."

Aulani nodded in approval and Cressida gave her a look. "And you are..."

"She's assisting Kalei with cultural preservation efforts," said Hoʻohuli quickly, so I wouldn't have to give our excuse. "And she's an esteemed guest of the king." Which meant she was under *my* protection, a protection I did not take lightly. Though Aulani did not know it, I sent guards to keep a watchful eye on her.

Cressida's gaze lingered too long, her lips curled. "How generous of you to help with that," she said to the mermaid. A servant refilled her goblet but she didn't drink. "It's no wonder you've delayed your coronation. You've been busy entertaining... guests."

My blood boiled. That was exactly what I *wanted* to do, but I couldn't, no thanks to her! She should be in prison, for all I cared.

Do you want me to spill this stew in her lap? I think it would make a statement. Aulani's refreshing voice in my head caused my anger to immediately decrease and a smirk tugged at my mouth. I straightened out.

"I delay public announcements," I said, "Because the truth should never be wrapped in politics."

Kalei choked slightly on her drink, and I knew she had hid a laugh, while Ho'ohuli nodded his approval. Cressida's expression didn't crack, but her hand tightened on her fork.

The breeze drifted in through the open lanai. From beneath the table, Pili chirped once and flitted toward Aulani. She plucked a piece of uala from her plate and fed the bird. When she looked at the bird, there was an undeniable energy in the room. It wasn't tense or electric, but rather calming, peaceful, and... healing.

And it was coming from Aulani.

Every head turned towards her as she petted Pili, looking at it as if she might be... communicating with it. The bird tweeted to her a few times and she smiled before lifting her finger and watching it fly out the door.

When she looked around, everyone quickly returned to their food. Everyone except Cressida. She watched with fascination, stared even.

And I did too. Aulani's eyes caught mine, and she winked. *It's not polite to stare, Ezra. If you were a merman, you'd know staring too long means you'll miss what's around you—and that's when a shark slips in from the deep.*

This time, I smiled, faintly. If only she knew. I wasn't afraid of a shark from the depths. I met with sharks every day—political ones—and sometimes the only way to endure them was to fix your gaze on something that reminded you that you weren't alone.

THE NEXT MORNING, I made up my mind: I had to see my people and visit the kingdom. And during that tour, I would take Aulani to the sea. I *promised* her, and already she'd been with us at least a week. She'd been so patient, but every day it killed me that I had not fulfilled my promise.

My coronation was in a few days, and Ho'ohuli said I should wait to become king before visiting the kingdom, but I was antsy to get out. I was antsy to see how my people *really* were doing.

I'd been in the palace discussing politics all day and resolving problems and issues, but I just needed to be among the natives and locals, and to observe the 'aina–the trees and wildlife–for myself.

Even more importantly, I needed to get Aulani to the sea.

As we got into the open carriage, I took the reins and Aulani sat next to me, her arm touching me. It was something I rather liked about her. I was not a "touchy" person, yet she never hesitated to sit close enough so our arms touched.

She was always so warm and smelled of the sea. Her hair, natural and wild in its own way, was down today and the energy from her felt like fresh mountain air compared to the tense meetings I'd been in the last while.

Kalei and Ho'ohuli joined us in the back of the wagon, and while Kalei began humming a song, Aulani smiled and sighed.

I wish I could sing with her, she said.

I wish you could too. I'm sad they'll never have a chance to hear your voice. I nudged her. *I'll admit I feel pretty lucky that your voice is all mine now though.*

Aulani nudged me back and laughed. *I like it when you say that.*

Say what?

That I'm yours. Her grin was infectious. I had to look away, my cheeks coloring.

Good. I didn't know what else to say, but when she moved even closer to me, I knew I was falling. I was falling fast and falling hard...

If I haven't already. I sighed quietly to myself. *Storms and surf, Ezra! Just stop! She's not from your world.* And if she didn't get back to Prince Ryker, she'd turn to sea foam. I couldn't let that happen.

We're taking her to the sea. Today.

Can I try? Aulani watched me hold the reins to the horses.

Sure. I handed them to her and nearly flipped backwards as she snapped the reins. The horses went off at a gallop, as if they found the mermaid amusing.

This was just a glimpse of the adventure in Aulani.

In the back, Kalei and Ho'ohuli laughed out loud–it was the first I'd heard Ho'ohuli laugh like that. He was always so stoic, and yet... he and Kalei were clutching the sides of the wagon for dear life, giggling and squealing like little kids. Aulani laughed too as we raced over a bridge, then she slowed the horses down, her hair a beautiful mess as the breeze picked up around us.

I couldn't help but put my hands behind my head and lean back. I don't know the last time I enjoyed myself... *really enjoyed* myself. But if this was the first–besides that one or two times I kissed Aulani–then I was going to be here, in this moment. Because these moments were like a cool breeze in the middle of a sweltering day. They didn't last long.

When we reached the village, the people rejoiced to see us. We still had a few more villages to go before the sea, but it took longer than I expected at each spot.

The children swarmed around Aulani like busy bees. At one point, we lost her because she'd gone off playing tag with the littles. They laughed and ran all over the town, my guards trying their best to be inconspicuous but keep an eye on Aulani who flitted around like a bird.

As I spoke with a village leader, some children came running to get their parents.

"You have to see the birds! They're back!" they exclaimed. My conversation died as I looked in the direction everyone was heading.

"It's Aulani!" Kalei exclaimed, running past me to see the commotion. As we neared the edge of the forest, a circle of people had formed around Aulani and the children. Big smiles crossed every child's face as each one took a turn around the mermaid princess.

"Who is she?" whispered the parents, but they didn't seem scared of her. They seemed amazed, like she was a miracle.

"The birds haven't sang like this since the coquis," said another.

"But they're singing... for her," said Hoʻohuli, his eyes wide as he looked from the princess to me. "She's not one of us, is she?" an old man whispered softly, and I shook my head.

A little child ran up to him, and everyone listened. "*Tutu kāne*! You should've seen what she did!" said the boy.

"What did she do?" the old man asked, placing a hand on his grandson's shoulder.

Others came closer to hear the child speak. Aulani and the other children were so entertained by the red honeycreeper, its curved beak entering in the flowers they fed it, that they didn't pay the adults any attention.

"Ioane found a bird at the edge of the forest. It was

dying, but when she held it, she did something... and then it jumped back up! Good as new!"

I blinked. I'd seen Aulani with birds. She told me what happened with Pili. But this... this could be the answer to losing our songbirds... because without them, our island was nothing. We were not Kaiora without our songbirds...

Tears filled the old man's eyes as he watched. Even Ho'ohuli was growing emotional.

Aulani could change our world. She could save it, even.

The boy ran back to the group to take his turn with the mermaid and the bird. "She's a miracle," said the old man.

Next to me, Ho'ohuli quietly spoke. "There was another like her... years ago."

I frowned. "What do you mean?"

Ho'ohuli moved his hand as if to emphasize Aulani's hair. "The hair. The striking eyes. She was a mystery but just her presence healed the songbirds, like this girl. She had hair like her–not red, but green. And some say she was the woman your father loved."

A lump formed in my throat. "Are you speaking of my mother?"

A nod. Nobody spoke of *my* mother. She was a foreigner, someone who literally came out of nowhere, then completely disappeared. Nobody knew where she came from or where she went.

Not even father would speak of mother. Only said we had the same eyes.

"You met her, didn't you?" I asked.

Ho'ohuli remained silent. Then, "Aulani could save our island... we need her, just as we needed your mother years ago."

Before I could ask any other questions, a guard drew Ho'ohuli's attention away.

My mother? Nobody had *ever* mentioned what she looked like, besides the fact she was a foreigner and I had her eyes.

I looked at the mermaid turned human, who now laughed, silently of course, with the children.

I need her. I swallowed hard. Our kingdom needed her.

No. I had to get her to the sea.

But as I looked at Aulani, I saw her with new eyes. She wasn't just a carefree mermaid who I'd grown affectionate towards. She was so much more... And Ho'ohuli was right. If she could not save our songbirds, who could?

As if to remind me of my current situation, a coqui chirped in the distance.

The coquis are taking over...

Shortly after Cressida announced herself ruler, she stopped hunting the coqui frogs. And because of that, they were growing at unprecedented rates again. Some were even mutating and becoming *larger* in size.

A soft breeze blew through the area, and I felt the ground beneath me humming, as if the island were speaking to me. It had been a while since I'd felt this, but the prompting was clear: *save the birds.*

I nodded to myself. As soon as we got back to the palace, I would put together an emergency council. The frogs needed to go.

Now.

And I wasn't Aulani's responsibility.

Something is bothering you. Aulani's attention turned to me. I nodded and she let the bird fly into the air, all watching with awe. *We should go back.*

I promised I'd take you to the sea today–

The birds are dying, Ezra. I can sense it. She gave me a serious look, and, despite all the people around us, it suddenly felt like it was only us. Alone. Looking into each other's eyes from a distance. There was something, deep inside of her, that meant she was bothered too.

Is something wrong, princess?

Of course. I can't go... not with your kingdom like this–

I can't ask that of you.

You didn't ask. I am choosing.

A child distracted her, but I sensed her coral walls strengthened, which meant one thing: she was hiding something from me.

THE STARS above Kaiora scattered like kalo in a lo'i, brilliant and numerous. I sat cross-legged on the flat stone of the terrace garden, my cloak tossed to one side. The night wind moved through my hair, carrying with it the musty scent of earth and stone.

I didn't turn when I heard the soft thump of sandals behind me.

"You always came here when life got unbearable." Kalei plopped herself beside me and handed over a carved wooden mug.

"I ran here because the palace walls have ears," I said.

She chuckled, folding her legs beneath her. "True. But also because this is where you think best. Here. On the earth. Surrounded by the wise old koa trees and cracked lava rock."

I took a long sip, the warm tea calming. "I'm supposed to be a good king, but I feel like I'm just rearranging coconuts in a sinking canoe."

"Coconuts float," Kalei said with a wink. "But I know what you mean."

We sat in silence for a while, the wind carrying with it

the echoes of the songbirds music that day. Pili swooped overhead before settling in the twisted branches of a nearby banyan tree.

"She's not like the others," I said finally, revealing what I'd *really* been thinking about.

"Aulani?"

I nodded.

"She's not from your world," my cousin said. She sighed. "But she sees it better than most who've lived in it their whole lives."

My voice was soft, maybe because I was afraid the wind might hear it and carry it to Aulani's ears. "I was a frog. She kissed me, saved me, helped me... and I keep thinking: what if I have to lose her to keep the kingdom?"

Kalei touched my arm. "Maybe this time, you don't choose what's expected. Maybe you choose what's right."

I didn't answer right away, just lifted my gaze to the stars and whispered, "If only I knew the difference."

CHAPTER TEN
AULANI

I always thought being a mermaid was confining, and that it set me apart from the rest of the world negatively. Ever since I was born, I'd always been able to communicate with animals and the world around me in a much deeper way than any other mermaids I knew.

The mermaids looked at me differently after that. They thought it was odd, and anytime I danced with the jellyfish, leaped with the dolphins, or sang to help the royal gardens grow, it set me farther and farther apart from the others.

Perhaps that's why I explored the surface world. The humans were *othered* by the mermaids, just like me. So perhaps that's where I belonged... with them.

I couldn't help but miss my little fish friend, Humu, and his loyalty even to my last splash in our world. And then Mo, my sister. She betrayed me, but what other choice did she have? I missed her, even as thoughts of her still stung bitterly.

But Aunt Lorelei thought differently of me.

When she saved me from the fisherman's net, she asked a nearby shark for help.

Mermaids mostly avoided sharks.

But she knew them.

She knew all the sea creatures and connected with them deeper than any mermaid I knew. I confessed to her about my strange connection to animals, and she said, “You have a gift, Aulani. Don’t hide it.”

And now that gift could bless this land, maybe even save it.

As much as I missed Humu and Mo, I knew I wouldn’t be seeing much of them whether in this world or our own.

And now that I’d been human for a few weeks, I was feeling more confused than ever before.

It was clear as day that the birds were dying from the frog infestation, and that something *had* to be done. Ezra sent out his troops every night to hunt the frogs, and he even went out himself, but the birds were dying of starvation. The balance on the land was not right.

The frogs are eating all the insects. Insects and bugs that the birds once relied on... I could sense the discouragement that the birds felt. They were losing in this frog battle, and if they were losing, the kingdom and island were losing. Ezra was losing.

But what if I could help?

I thought of this as I watched the coronation.

Crowned King of Kaiora, Ezra looked magnificent. The newly crowned king stood before his people, his expression stoic, green eyes somber, crown sparkling.

"I hereby declare you, Ezra Keoki Kanahele, as the Sovereign King of Kaiora, Keeper of the songbirds, and Protector of the ‘Aina." People threw flowers into the air, filling it with rich floral scents.

And despite being in the crowd with Kalei, I thought Ezra wouldn’t see us. But his eyes searched until he found me, and a smile gently touched his lips. My heart burst as I clapped my hands.

I wished I could cheer with the others.

Festivities began almost immediately after, and while Kalei ran off to try the food, I stood by a pillar, watching Ezra. He was a perfect king. The perfect person to rule Kaiora, especially.

He must have felt my eyes on him because, when he finally had a moment, he stole away behind the pillar. A confusing mix of excitement and sadness swirled inside of me, a whirlpool that seemed to sink right into the depths of my heart: Excitement because he was finally king, but sadness because, well, I was going to have to leave at some point...

And I'll never see him again. I brushed the thought away as he hurried towards me, extending his arms. I threw my arms around his neck, and he spun us around, his own arms around my back. It was magical, and I wished we could stay in this dazzling, warm, protective embrace forever.

You did it, Ezra! You are king! I squeezed him extra tight, taking in his fresh scent that was like rain and cedarwood and musky earth.

I couldn't have done it without you! Ezra wasn't one to exclaim things, but the happiness that came from his mind to mine was light, like buoyant foam on the surface of the sea.

All I can say is congratulations, my frog prince–now king! I laughed at that.

As he set me down, he kept his hands on my waist, and my hands slipped onto his hard, warm chest. The pillar, large foliage, and ferns hid us well, and I deeply wanted to kiss him.

Aulani! Oh, kelp *me, I was falling for him!* What a forbidden thought!

His eyes sparkled as they looked into mine, and from the color on his cheeks, I wondered if he thought the same thing.

A smile crossed my lips, and he returned the favor, the air charged between us. I looked at his lips, remembering the last two times we kissed. He was *perfect* for me...

I knew I shouldn't, especially since I would not be in this realm forever, but I leaned in. He leaned in too, a silence before a storm, knowing that this safety and calm would not last forever, but we had to enjoy while we could...

Just as his lips were about to touch mine, his warm breath on my skin...

"Ezra, where did you–"

We jumped apart at the sound of Hoʻohuli's voice. He blushed, having seen us in our intimate position, our faces close together. We all blushed, actually, and Ezra rubbed the back of his neck. His cheeks bloomed like coral under moonlight.

Hoʻohuli gave the king a look, and I had the briefest notion that they had discussed me. It was almost a warning look, but one that was also full of sympathy: even Hoʻohuli knew I couldn't stay here.

"Ezra, Lord and Lady Kawai'ae'a are leaving soon and wished to bid you congratulations before their departure."

The king nodded, regaining his composure quickly, while I stood there feeling dejected and disappointed. *Perfect timing, Hoʻohuli...*

Instead, I turned to Ezra and nodded encouragingly. *You have so many people to talk to. I'm truly happy for you, Ezra. You are going to be the best king this kingdom has ever had.* It was as if he wanted to say *so* much more, but instead, he nodded.

Thank you, Aulani. With that, he bowed, turned on his heels, and followed Ho'ohuli, leaving me alone.

"I saw that." I jumped to find Kalei approaching, a plate of food in her hands. We watched her cousin as he talked to his people, a kind smile on his face, as if he had put a certain distraction out of his mind. His wandering eyes betrayed him though, and when he saw us watching him, his lip twitched and looked away quickly. My heart skipped a beat.

"He doesn't want to lose you," Kalei said softly. "But he will... he has to. You're not from our world, and if you don't get back to yours *and* your prince, you'll die."

I sighed, and, for the first time since I'd arrived, I realized I did *not* want to go back to my world. What if I stayed? What if things worked out between Ezra and me? The more time I spent with him, the more I *wanted* it all to work out.

Because if I stay, I will *die.* I had to get Prince Ryker to fall in love with me, or I'd turn to sea foam. Those were the terms of the curse. Anger boiled inside me. I had no choice... I had to resist Ezra.

I need to get to the sea, I said softly to Ezra, and he met my eyes.

Yes. I'll take you.

Tonight?

Yes. I promise. And I knew he intended to keep that promise, no matter what.

I STARED at the stars as I waited for Ezra. Where was he? He said to meet at the stables, but it was getting dark. Had something delayed him?

You're acting like a seal being chased by a whale, Aulani. Calm down, I told myself, and tried to think about the telescope I saw in Prince Ryker's jacket. When I returned to my world, I would get him to fall in love with me, marry me, and I could ask him all the questions about the stars.

I can forget all about Kaiora, the frogs, the birds, and... him. Ezra. That made me sadder than a shipwreck without treasure.

I don't want to forget him. Ezra was the sweetest person I'd ever met. He never judged. He just saw me for who I was...

And where is he?

Anxiety pressed on me as doubts formed. What if Ezra would not take me to the sea?

He wouldn't lie to me. He just wasn't that kind of a person. Ezra was honest and genuine to the core.

Suddenly, our mind connection brimmed with life, like Ezra was trying to reach out to me. The connection felt tangled though, like a fishing line snagged on something.

We could only communicate when we were within a certain proximity, but it felt as if he was far away from me... and getting farther and farther.

Ezra? I stepped away from the stable, my heart beginning to race.

Aulani! He spoke in a panicked voice.

Where are you?

Nothing. Fear gripped me, and I began running. I didn't know where, just... I had to move.

Ezra! I screamed in my mind, rushing through the palace walls.

"Is everything all right?" Ho'ohuli asked, and I shook my head, trying to tell him Ezra was in trouble, but he didn't understand. I ran off, and he trailed behind me.

Ezra, where are you? Again, nothing. I couldn't even sense his mind, which frightened me even more.

And then... ever so faintly...

The garden... I'm...

Nothing...

I rushed to the garden at the front of the palace, passing the gardeners cleaning up their landscaping tools for the day. Someone cut the rose bushes to perfection.

"Aulani!" Ho'ohuli was still following me. "What is going on?"

The garden? I shook my head. Where could he be in the garden?

Wrong garden! I told myself, and looked to the back of the palace, where the terrace garden grew wild and free. Yes. He went there often to be alone. I darted in that direction, Ho'ohuli out of breath behind me.

"Slow down, Aulani!" he called, but I couldn't.

Wouldn't.

Ezra was in trouble, and I needed to help him.

When I reached the terrace garden, the sound of a coqui frog filled the air.

Ezra! I climbed the lava rock terraces, avoiding stepping in the middle as saplings and young plants grew within. As I reached the top, panic began settling in. He was not anywhere in sight.

Ezra. I couldn't sense him. Couldn't see his koa trees blocking his mind from my view. Couldn't sense his warm, calm presence in my mind. An unsettling feeling came over me. If I couldn't sense his mind, was his mind... dark? Was he... gone?

I slumped to my knees as water pooled in my eyes. *Where are you Ezra?* What happened to him? Was I too late?

A coqui frog chirped nearby and I swallowed hard. *Ezra, I'm so sorry...*

"Don't be." I jumped, aware that he spoke to me, but his mind seemed so far, so empty, so... small? Even his voice was quiet.

Ezra, where are you? I looked around in the darkness, hoping to see his form approach. Instead, he said, "I need you to kiss me again."

This isn't a time to joke. Where are you?

"I've been trying to get your attention."

I frowned and continued to search the area. *If I had a sand dollar for each time you tell me information without telling me anything, I could buy your whole kingdom,* I said rather angrily.

Aulani, look down. He spoke to my mind.

I did, but then I had to kneel because, well...

You're a frog again? I wanted to scream. *Who did this to you?*

Can you kiss me so I can transform into a human first? The little thing coqui-ed and it echoed around us.

Ho'ohuli arrived at that moment, bending over, hands on his knees as he struggled to catch his breath. I waved to him, trying to explain that the little coqui in my hand was Ezra, but his face was red and his eyes were wide. He understood nothing I tried to explain with my hands.

Just kiss me already, Ezra said, adding, *Please.*

I wished he would say that to me when he wasn't a frog in need of turning back into a king.

I could if you wanted me to. Ezra heard me, his tone both humorous and bitter. *Kissing humans is much better than kissing frogs, I'm sure.*

I rolled my eyes and kissed him. This time, I watched. The air around us grew electric, tense even, like a coiled tide ready to break. Golden magic swirled around the frog and it grew until a young man crouched in front of me, his green eyes warm as our faces were close to each other.

He looked at my lips. I looked at his.

"Ezra!" Ho'ohuli exclaimed, shocked as he made his way up the terraces. "Whatever happened? You were a *frog* again?"

"I came here to get a flower–" He paused as the tips of his ears turned red. A flower? Then I realized... he got a flower for me.

A million feelings erupted inside of me, like a sea volcano ready to burst and touch the surface. "Anyway, all I remember is on my way here, things started getting blurry and by the time I reached the garden, I was a frog again."

"What? How?" Ho'ohuli was speechless. "*Who*? Was there anyone around you?"

"Not that I recall."

What were you doing before you came to the garden?

"I was seeing Princess Cressida off."

Ho'ohuli and I exchanged looks and he folded his arms. "You don't think it was her, do you?"

Ezra shrugged. "Now that I think of it, she *was* the last person I saw before I turned into a frog both times."

"Where are your guards?" Ho'ohuli said.

"I asked them to wait inside the palace, like they normally do when I come to the terrace garden."

But my mind was on Cressida. *The ball,* I said. *Did she have that golden ball?* I recalled him telling me about the ball.

"Her hands were concealed in the jacket she held over her arms..." Ezra frowned. "Maybe she could've been holding it?"

It has to have magic! I shook my head. *You can't let her leave! She should be under arrest for questioning.*

"You're right." Ezra looked at Ho'ohuli. "Stop Cressida from leaving. She is summoned for questioning about the frog curse, and a fair trial must take place for her crimes against Kaiora. We'll have the trial sooner than I planned."

"Right away." Ho'ohuli bowed, took a breath, then ran off.

Which left Ezra and I alone, something that filled me with anticipation and excitement. He let his legs dangle off the edge of the terrace and I joined him, scooting closer so our arms touched.

We should get going, he said, but he didn't move. He played with a blade of grass in his hand, his eyebrows furrowed, like he was distracted by the frog situation. I couldn't blame him, and, suddenly, I wanted to figure it all out before reaching the sea and getting back to my world...

What was the flower for? I asked, even though I knew very well what it was for.

The corner of Ezra's lip turned up. Instead of answering, he said, *I spoke to Ho'ohuli in the village the other day. He said he's seen someone like you before, years ago. She couldn't speak, but her hair was tinted like yours, and just her presence seemed to bring life to the birds and the trees.*

I tipped my head. Someone, like me, was here? In this world? Were there mermaids in Ezra's sea after all? I supposed we'd find out soon enough...

Ho'ohuli knows an old man familiar with magic, and when I asked if he could alter spells and curses, he said he could try. But a sea witch's magic is more powerful than anything else...

Why was Ezra saying this?

His magic encompasses transformations, even... Ezra swallowed, as if he was unsure what to say next. *He might be able to... alter your spell. Not reverse it. But change it... so you can stay.*

My breath caught. *Stay?* My voice barely carried, like a tired wind over the sea's surface.

With me. Ezra's eyes locked on mine, his cheeks rosy even in the glimmering moonlight. *If you wanted.*

My entire world lit up, like watching coral flowers bloom and blossom on a warm, sunny day.

Ezra... I was speechless, which was something for a mute girl who could only communicate with her mind.

I'm not just asking if you'll stay, the king continued, his voice deep and certain, like he was rooted in his decision. He reached for my hand and clasped it. *I'm asking if you'll marry me. If we can make this work, and if the spell can be shaped to fit the future instead of erasing the past, will you be mine?*

I smiled so wide, it hurt. *Yes.* I barely breathed as tears blurred my vision. *Yes! I want that. I want you!*

I threw my arms around him, nearly causing him to fall back. He caught himself though and wrapped his arms around me. Our eyes locked, every breath pulsing with energy and life.

But before our lips met, Ezra pulled back. *We should probably wait... We don't know if he can do the magic or not. I just... I want you to stay, but if not...* Then kissing would make it harder.

I nodded and squeezed his hand.

Footsteps thundered from the path as a voice cut through the night. "Ezra!"

Ho'ohuli interrupts everything, I thought, rather annoyed. He was like a nurse shark lingering at the bottom of the water, choosing to move at the most inconvenient times.

We broke apart before the man appeared. Guards and Kalei came pounding behind him.

"What's going on?" Ezra stood, then helped me up, taking my hand in his.

"He's back," Kalei exclaimed as Hoʻohuli tried to catch his breath. He'd been running quite a bit. I looked from the old man's red face to Kalei, who was pale as a white pearl.

"Ezra," she said. Her eyes pooled with tears. "He's alive, Ezra. Tavo. He's alive, and he's brought an army."

But something shattered the moment, and Ezra's hand never left mine. Just when it seemed like everything was going to be alright, it unraveled, like a kelp strand caught in a shifting current, pulled loose and drifting, unable to anchor itself.

CHAPTER ELEVEN
EZRA

I didn't take her to the sea. When would I ever keep my promise? It was killing me. But she'd have to wait... just a moment longer.

Because Tavo is back. It felt like the wind had blown down a steady koa tree, one that had just taken root, one that had just grounded and believed nothing could cause it to up heave. And yet... the news came so suddenly and forcefully, I stood there holding my breath, for, what felt like, hours.

"Ezra." Kalei shook my shoulders. I sucked in air.

This is all too much... He was... dead. And now?

"He's on his way to the palace now," my cousin said. "I think people are wondering what's going to happen–word has already spread that he's alive. People at the ports are celebrating."

Celebrating? Had they celebrated when I came back from being a frog?

Ezra, we should go. Aulani touched my arm and I met her eyes, this woman who I wanted to marry–and who wanted to marry me. Yes. She was beside me. *I'll be with you,* she said, and my heart stilled. Only for a moment.

We went to the throne room, where I paced, waiting. Aulani, Hoʻohuli, my other closest counselors, and Kalei stood off to the side, along with my guards. Cressida was being escorted back to the palace, and Tavo would be here any minute.

"Why would he bring an army?" I asked aloud, fists clenched. I wanted to welcome back my brother, I really did. But all of this seemed... off. He was *dead.* Dead, with a capital D. His men brought back his *leiomano* and said he died in foreign lands, coming face to face in a duel with a white man.

"How did he survive?" I hated it appeared I was angry about this. There was no anger in me though, just confusion. I was *glad* my brother was alive, yet, at the same time, incredibly worried.

I was just crowned... And he comes home, right *after* that happened? Was he hoping to take the throne? Come back and claim what was supposed to be his? Would there be a power struggle?

Just as I could wait no longer, the throne doors opened and in strode a man worn by the sea.

Tavo was always bigger and bulkier than me, but he was just as tall. With his wavy dark black hair pulled back into a bun, he looked as robust as ever.

"Little brother!" he exclaimed and rushed to me. I hugged my brother, still confused.

"You're alive," was all I said, then relief flooded me at the truth of that statement. I relaxed a little. "You're alive, Tavo." He held my shoulders as we pulled apart.

"What happened?" I asked, amazed. Tavo and I didn't exactly look like brothers. He had dark brown skin like the natives, and his eyes were the color of dark eucalyptus. He looked every bit like the king of Kaiora, a full-blooded native...

"I survived," Tavo said, his voice rough yet assertive.

"How? They said you died in a duel. They brought back your leiomano."

"My men turned against me."

I gaped. "The soldiers who brought back your weapon? They said nothing of a mutiny..."

Tavo's eyes narrowed at the word "mutiny."

"It wasn't a mutiny." His tone had an edge to it.

I stiffened. "Then why would they turn on you?"

He walked up to the throne–my throne–and sat on it lazily, swinging his bulky legs over the armrest and putting his hands behind his head, as if he didn't have a care in the world.

"Tavo..." I didn't want to get impatient, but it was apparent: he was hiding something. His men–our people and guards who were loyal to us–wouldn't just *turn* on him.

There had to be a reason.

And, now that I thought of it, the men who returned Tavo's weapon retired and disappeared. They told us that he died in foreign lands but never provided enough details. Only, "He was shot."

"I felt burdened," Tavo said, staring at the ceiling. "Perhaps my stress caused my men to betray me. We were in foreign lands. They took me to a gang who shot me. They thought they killed me, but I healed and waited until I could return home."

I should have sympathized with him. While he was struggling for his life in a land far from ours, I was struggling for my life as a frog.

And now we were *both* back.

He smiled, and in that smile, my stomach twisted. "In my journey to return home, I realized what an honor I was given," said my brother. "I'm back."

"Ezra Keoki is the king of Kaiora," Ho'ohuli said, stepping in. "We welcome you, Tavo, but your brother has already been crowned."

Tavo tipped his chin to me. "Of course." His tone was bitter. "I do command armies, and I have befriended many foreign powers who have their eyes on our beloved kingdom."

Our beloved kingdom? Was he... threatening me?

"How did you get an army?" I asked, and Tavo sat up... finally. He was rather embarrassing us both by laying like a beached whale on the throne. I was glad I didn't have to scold him in front of everyone. This was awkward enough as it was.

"I used my influence. Convinced and persuaded people to follow me." He grinned at me. "We can make Kaiora the most powerful kingdom in the world, Ezra."

Someone shifted uncomfortably and that's when Tavo's attention turned. He noticed our cousin, Kalei, next to Ho'ohuli and they kissed one another's cheeks.

"Welcome back," she said quietly, then added, "It's like we're seeing a ghost, Tavo..."

"Don't worry Kalei." He waved his hand at her. "I'm as real as ever." His eyes then latched onto Aulani, standing there, observing him. She didn't flinch under his gaze, but held it.

"Who's this pretty little lady?" He approached her and that's when I stepped in.

"She's mine, Tavo."

"Ah." He recoiled quickly, nostrils slightly flared.

I don't trust him. Aulani's voice said to me and I couldn't agree more. I'd never been close to my brother, with the biggest reason being our blood. He saw me as inferior for my half-blooded heritage.

And now he's the one gallivanting with the foreigners...

My brother turned his attention back to me. "I am willing to discuss politics, Ezra. And to discuss the matter of the throne."

So he does want the throne back.

I swallowed hard. "We can discuss things tomorrow," I said. "It's late and a lot has happened today."

"Of course, your majesty." He was mocking me. I could see it in his eyes.

Ho'ohuli then stepped in, telling Tavo where he could stay in the palace. My nobles and counselors looked from me to Tavo, and that's when I *felt* it. A shift. They were deciding which leader they saw more suitable for the throne, and at least half of them probably thought it was him.

Your people believe in you. Aulani's voice sounded, as if she could read my thoughts.

You don't understand, Aulani. He was raised to be king his whole life. These people have looked to him as the sovereign ruler. I've never been enough.

Her eyebrows furrowed. *You are enough, Ezra. You are the greatest king this people has ever seen.*

I blocked my wary thoughts from her.

No. I was not a good enough king, especially not without her. *She* would be the answer to saving our island, and, though I had proposed to her and made it clear that I wanted to be with her, that was another reason I wanted–no, needed–her to stay.

I should tell her. But would she feel like I was using her?

Everything felt so fragile in that moment, I wished I

could be in my garden again... away from everyone and everything.

Cressida stepped into the room, and when she saw Tavo, her entire expression changed. It was strange to see...

Perhaps she really did love him.

"You're alive!" She ran to him and threw her arms around his neck. They were a strong contrast: her white, pale skin and pastel colored dress against his dark brown skin and black sailing suit. Much to my relief, they didn't kiss in front of everyone. I'd seen them kiss before, and relief filled me that I wouldn't have to witness that again. "I thought you were gone."

Tavo held her, but I saw a flash of doubt in his eyes, as if he weren't sure he really wanted to hold her.

"I missed you so much," she breathed, and an audible "aww" quietly passed through the room.

I think she's lying. Aulani's voice cut straight to my mind and, in the midst of the tension, thick as poi before adding water, I had to hold back a laugh. She must've caught onto the fact it was funny, because she added, *I'd rather face a sea serpent in a hurricane than have to endure watching this.*

I quickly stood a little straighter, grateful for Aulani's distraction. As long as I had her intrusive thoughts, I told myself I'd be fine.

I ANNOUNCED a welcome home banquet the following day, so the palace was busy with preparations for that, and I had meetings to attend. Cressida was going to be brought in for questioning, and Tavo wanted to attend my political meetings.

But I denied him entrance.

I had to speak with my counselors and advisors *alone.*

Partway through the day, I invited him in, and what he wanted to do blew me away.

He wanted to bring in foreigners to cultivate the land, raise more plantations and crops, and completely change our government to mirror that of others' structures. There were some aspects of it I liked, but others? Well... it just felt like he was abandoning *our* ways, and trying to control the land. There was no sense of respect for the 'aina, no acknowledgement or even desire to preserve it, protect it, and cultivate it for generations to come.

He was like the businessmen who came to our islands, who only had gold in their eyes. Essentially, he wanted to turn our kingdom into a factory that then pumped out sugarcane, pineapple, and other exotic fruits and goods to ship off to other lands.

I was all about trade, but only at a wise and steady pace, one that respected our land and people.

"We're going to allow foreigners in at *our* pace," I finally said, cutting Tavo off. Half of the room was listening with interest, while the other half looked relieved at my interruption. "I dismiss you, Tavo."

He slammed his fist on the table. "Stop wasting time, Ezra! If you cared about our people and our island, you would bring in the snakes to get rid of the frogs, build up plantations, modernize with the times, and trade with foreign markets!"

Silence. I took a slow, quiet breath and looked around. "I think we've been in meetings long enough today. The meeting is adjourned till tomorrow."

With that, I stood and approached my brother. His jaw clenched. "Listen to me, Ezra," he said so only I could hear. "You *may* have had the luck of being given the throne, but it belongs to me. *I* know how to rule this people. You never learned. Father wanted *me* to rule."

"Did you visit father's grave?" I asked. After father's death became known, people erected a memorial. I'd visited it several times since coming back from my frog form.

Tavo let out a breath.

Of course he hadn't visited father's grave.

Our conversation today was done. He shook his head and strode out.

I UNFASTENED the clasp at my throat and let the yellow and red feathered cloak fall. It was too hot for this time of year, and felt much too heavy. Everything felt heavy.

They're siding with him. I could see it in the eyes of my counselors and advisors. Tavo spoke of alliances like trade and people like numbers. I hated how diplomacy tasted like swallowing sea salt.

The wind was cooler here beneath the kukui tree. Its leaves rustled softly, silver undersides flashing in the island breeze. My grandfather planted it, and I used to sit beneath it as a boy, believing if I sat still long enough, it would whisper my grandfather's wisdom to me.

But there was nothing. Not today. Not ever, really.

Grandfather probably liked Tavo better.

Your majesty. A sing-songy, bright voice came from behind the low garden wall. *You're going to wrinkle your face if you keep frowning like that. Is that how kings get old so fast?*

I didn't turn. *No. We earn them from kissing mermaids.*

She hopped over the wall–graceful as ever, barefoot and wild-haired–and plopped beside me like we were children. I didn't stop her. I never did.

You were more hop-ful when you were a frog, she teased.

I was quieter then.

You still are.

I gave her a sideways glance. *The funny thing is, I had a longer tongue.*

She burst into laughter: loud, bright, and echoing off the walls in my mind. I let myself smile... just a little. She nudged my shoulder with hers. *What's weighing you down, frog prince?*

I sighed and looked out towards the lush mountains, which leveled out until they met the sea in the far distance. "Foreign kings trying to buy my people's loyalty like it's fruit at a market. They offer wealth, weapons, women..." I shook my head. "All to 'help' us, bribe us while cutting our roots."

Oh you mean Tavo.

I sighed and nodded. The fact that he offered *people* as a form of trade made me sick to my stomach. He spoke of paper brides and indentured servants, even slaves. I could never do that... not to my people. Not to anyone.

You're not just their king, you know, she said softly, her gaze tracking the wind-blown ti leaves. *You're the protector of this island and every life within it.*

I looked at her then. Really looked at her. Her hair smelled like hibiscus and sea salt, and she had a smear of dirt on her cheek, like she'd been exploring again. Pili, that ridiculous songbird, circled above us and then landed on her shoulder. He watched me with tilted eyes.

And you, I said dryly, *are the mermaid who talks to birds and stole my heart.*

She grinned. *You stole mine first, frog boy.*

We sat in silence for a while, then I whispered to myself, "My kuleana feels heavier every day."

Aulani reached over without ceremony and took my hand, calloused from planting and pen alike. *Then let me carry some of it. Just for a while. I've got strong arms.* She squeezed my hand. *Mermaid arms.*

I blinked down at our hands and interlaced our fingers, watching as the shimmer of sunlight danced across our skin.

That's not how mermaids work. I thought they were all dainty and put together.

You've clearly never met one like me.

This time, I laughed.

CHAPTER TWELVE
AULANI

The welcome banquet was quite the scene. Ezra spared no expenses in making sure his brother was welcome home while asserting his position as king. Ezra sat at the head of the table, with me sitting on his right side, and Tavo lounging on his left side.

In this position, I felt that I was in a rather uncomfortable spot because Tavo kept staring at me. He was trying to figure me out, trying to understand why Ezra had a mute girl next to him, especially a girl who did not look like anyone else here. Among my other unique features, my red-tinted hair stood out like a red anemone in a bed of pale shells. I wore blue, while everyone here wore earthy tones of browns, muted creams and ivories, and lots of green.

Cressida sat at the farthest end of the table. Earlier that day, they questioned her, but she pleaded innocent to everything... or so Ezra told me. I didn't trust her, and I wondered if they had asked her about that golden ball...

The banquet table glittered with candlelight and crystal, gold leafing curling along the rims of koa wood goblets and plates like vines. Music trickled through the high-vaulted ceilings, and laughter echoed from every corner–except where Ezra sat.

Everyone was happy to have *both* brothers back, but neither brother seemed too pleased to see each other. The tension between them was taut and uncomfortable.

Across from me, Tavo sipped from his goblet and let his eyes rake slowly over me. My eyebrows furrowed. "Ezra," he said, smiling as smooth as oil on water. "You've brought quite the enchantress to the table. What was your name again, love?"

Love? I lifted my chin as my fingers tightened on my fork.

Ezra's jaw flexed. "She doesn't speak," he said.

Tavo clicked his tongue. "What a shame. So beautiful, yet... so quiet." He grinned. "The best treasures often are." He leaned forward, and my insides tightened. "What was her name again?"

Ezra's grip tightened around his goblet. "Her name is Aulani."

"Aulani." Tavo said my name, as if he were tasting it in his mouth. "Interesting. She doesn't look like she's from here." I hated he was talking about me *right in front of me.* Ezra, too, seemed completely bothered by this.

Want my fist to smash his nose?

I nearly laughed aloud at Ezra's intrusive thought, and when he met my eyes, they sparkled. Despite the gleam in them, though, he also looked worried, and I sensed the undercurrent of insecurity within him.

"What is she anyway?" Tavo asked. "A garden girl? A hula dancer?"

"She's none of your concern," Ezra said coolly.

Tavo raised an eyebrow. "Touchy, brother. I only meant

to appreciate the mystery... unless you're hiding something."

Ezra ignored him, and when I met Tavo's eyes, he studied me. It wasn't the kind of look I'd say was an admirable look, but rather...

What if he uses me against Ezra? Was I going to make things more complicated? Considering his burdens, would he crack under the pressure if another one was added?

Tavo raised his goblet to me, unconcerned. "If you tire of Ezra's mood, dear lady, I'd be more than happy to–"

"She's not interested." Ezra snapped finally, his words sharp enough to silence the nearby conversations. Ho'ohuli and Kalei exchanged worried glances and a hush fluttered over our section of the table.

Tavo's eyes narrowed, though his smirk remained. "Careful, Ezra. You're starting to sound like father."

"Maybe I want to be more like father," Ezra said, and I slipped my hand under the table, resting it lightly on Ezra's leg. His hand found mine and he squeezed it.

Tavo turned away, lips twitching with whatever unspoken game he thought he was winning. But Ezra... he seemed unearthed. He seemed... *mad.* I'd never seen this expression on him, or felt it from him. He was always so calm. Grounded. Steady.

But this... this was a different side of Ezra, and I worried for him.

LATER THAT NIGHT, I stood on the rooftop of the palace, gazing at the stars.

Thinking about the telescope I found in Ryker's pocket... and Mo, Humu, and the world I left behind. I missed it and wondered what would happen when I returned, but I worried deeply about Ezra.

"I thought I'd find you here."

I turned to see Ezra approach. Ezra's tunic was unbuttoned and open, which showed some of his muscled chest underneath, and his hair looked messy, as if he'd run his fingers through it. I had to look away, my heart pounding.

As much as I wanted to imagine a life here with Ezra, the old man who knew magic hadn't had much luck the past couple of days. He came by to tell Ezra he still couldn't find any spells or magic in Kaiora that could help me.

I sighed, focusing on the moment at hand. *I love the stars, Ezra. You can see them so well here in the mountains.*

Ezra leaned against the railing and I joined him, our arms touching. I always loved his warmth.

You don't have to pretend he didn't get to you, the king finally said, his voice tight. *He's charming. Powerful.* He exhaled. *He's everything I'm not.*

Ezra... Tavo was the *last* thing I was thinking about. If anything, my thoughts now turned to Cressida and the frog situation. I should've been thinking about the sea and my days wearing thin. But there was so much to do here, and I desperately wanted to help Ezra... I wanted to take just *one* thing off his plate.

I should let you go, Aulani. Maybe it's selfish to want you to stay when I can't even promise–He looked down at the view below, stopping himself. *You looked so far away tonight.*

I touched his hand and our fingers intertwined, as if they were used to doing this. Ezra looked at me with his green eyes, eyes that looked so sad and tired. Worn down.

My fingers brushed his smooth cheek, then trailed down his jaw.

If you didn't catch my drift, you're slower than a sea slug in molasses, Ezra.

He barked a laugh, sudden and real and relieved. *You hated him.*

I gave a single nod, solemn as the moon on the sea, then pulled him down so our foreheads touched. He closed his eyes and I felt something in him–something raw and aching and afraid.

I don't want to lose you. His voice was soft. Gentle. *Not to him. Not to the sea. Not to anything.*

I gently kissed his cheek, falling into his fresh koa wood scent.

Then you better keep your promise, I teased and he wrapped his arms around me, holding me close.

What if we did *find a way to permanently transform you to a human? Would your heart swim away and I never see you again?*

I grinned. *What if I dragged you with me?*

He laughed again, something I counted as a victory. *You're dangerous, mermaid, you know that?*

Only for you, I said and hugged him. No kisses... not yet.

I COULDN'T SLEEP. Even after spending a romantic moment under the stars with Ezra, I tossed and turned. Not only was the sea calling to me, but something just didn't feel right.

Magic.

I could no longer resist the tingling sensation in the air. Someone was using magic, and it wasn't the comforting, cozy magic that Aunty Lorelei used, nor was it the natural magic that existed in the forest's life or the songbirds.

It was a leeching kind of magic that made the air feel

heavy. I wasn't exactly familiar with *dark* magic, per se, but I was pretty sure this was it.

Where is it coming from? I got out of bed, changed, and slowly made my way into the hallway, tiptoeing barefoot, following my instincts. I walked out of the palace, and Pili circled before landing on my shoulder. He shook his feathers, as if nervous for me, as if telling me to turn around and go back.

But I didn't want to go back. I had to find whatever was causing this imbalance in the air, and I had to stop it.

The coquis were ridiculously loud, so loud it almost made it difficult for me to sense the tingling, pulsing sensation in the air. I passed through the terrace garden, traversing deep into the forest.

The koa trees were so old they seemed to hold the wisdom of thousands of years. No wonder the people loved these forests, these trees. They had a life all their own. Tavo spoke of cutting them down, and that made my heart ache.

The locals cut them down too, I told myself. Yes, this was true. They used the wood for ships and weapons... but Tavo meant to cut them down at an *alarming* rate.

Ezra won't let that happen. He cared for his people, this land, and these trees. A coqui chirped next to me and I jumped, eyeing it with suspicion.

Not Ezra. The normal coquis were a dull color, like white sand mixed with ashes from a campfire. Ezra, in his frog form, had had more of a green color, with a golden tint, as if he were still wearing his green kingly tunics even in frog form.

Suddenly, the air became more charged, and I felt a stinging sensation inside my chest. The trees were sinking—not physically, but the life in them was drifting away to something unseen, something terrifying.

Even the birds and owls hid in the trees, but they could not escape the magic force, sucking their lives like a whirlpool dragging the surrounding water, drawing everything to its center.

That's when I saw a light. I moved, careful not to step on any branches or rustle any leaves. With skirts hiked up above my knees, I crouched behind a large monstera bush.

My jaw dropped.

In the center of the opening was a light, and it came not from a lantern nor a fire. It came from a ball.

A golden ball.

Cressida. She held it in her hands, trying to conceal the light from the forest, yet it still glowed.

What is she doing? Black magic drifted like ribbons in the air, connecting itself from the trees and nearby life to the ball.

The ball is taking the life from the trees, the birds, and... Not the frogs. No. Coquis hopped around, and even if I had made a sound, they were so much louder. Their endless, annoying chirping hurt my ears.

Cressida suddenly paused and looked around, as if scared someone might find her here. I ducked, knowing she couldn't see me, but hoping she wouldn't detect my presence.

Something rustled in the bushes nearby and the princess jumped up, covering the ball with her dark cloak. "Who's there?" Her voice trembled, and her fingers shook.

A mongoose scurried across the opening, and she pressed a hand against her heart, her face pale with fear. Then she let out a breath and knelt down, the ball no longer glowing.

Cressida whispered some words.

A spell? Aunty Lorelei had said a spell to activate my potion. How was this any different?

The golden ball takes magic from the natural inhabitants of the island. The coquis are not from here, so it doesn't take from them... I gaped. *But this ball... it turns people to frogs!*

And that was all I needed to know. I had my evidence. I had seen everything I needed to see. Part of me wanted to dash into the clearing, grab the ball, and run away so I could destroy it, but I hesitated.

What if she turns me *into a frog?* I couldn't risk that. I'd tell Ezra. Now.

I tiptoed back, my heart racing, hoping she would not see or hear me. But, of course, I tripped on a root. The leaves and twigs cracked and rustled beneath me. I internally cursed.

Oh, squid ink!

"Who's there?" Cressida's voice sounded again, and this time, she was moving. So I was moving. I bolted away into the darkness, hearing her call after me. "Stop!"

She didn't see me, right? She didn't recognize me, right?

I didn't stop running, tripping, and getting back up until I reached the palace. I was still ridiculously clumsy with these legs. When I reached the terrace garden, I slipped behind a pile of barrels, close to the palace walls, to catch my breath. After a moment, I dared to look in the direction I came, but there was nobody. Perhaps Cressida gave up trying to catch me.

Slipping out of the shadows, I moved towards the palace, nodding to the guards who eyed my sweaty face with raised eyebrows.

Ezra. I had to tell him. Now.

I was right.

Cressida turned him into a frog! She had to be arrested.

As I turned the corner, my stomach sank like an anchor dropping quickly into the water.

Tavo stood at the end of the covered walkway, his back turned towards me. I darted behind the nearest pillar, silently disappearing behind a bush of large monstera leaves.

Tavo didn't even notice. Didn't even look.

As far as I knew, he wasn't aware of my presence.

In fact, he looked like he was waiting for someone. Footsteps sounded through the covered walkway and a man appeared.

Fair skin. Fair hair. Blue eyes.

The man was a fish out of water amongst the brown-skinned natives.

"Well?" Tavo folded his arms, his back still towards me. "Who is she?"

"It's true," the man said, and Tavo shook his head, turning around and rubbing his chin.

I crouched lower in the bush, listening.

"So she's not from here... then what is she hiding? Does she have Ezra under a spell?"

"She can't talk... so how could her song put the king under a trance?" asked the man, and I realized he and Tavo were talking about, well, *me!*

"Mermaids..." Tavo shook his head. "How did Ezra catch a mermaid?"

My eyes widened. How did he know? We hadn't told anyone... except Kalei and Ho'ohuli...

Did they betray us? The sting was worse than a jellyfish burn and I shuddered.

"I can take her back to her world," said Tavo, thinking aloud. "Make her trust me. Ezra is probably lying to her about taking her to the sea."

"Why would he do that?" asked the man, confused.

"Same reason father tried to trap Ezra's mother."

Ezra's mother? What is he talking about? I shook my head and Tavo ran his fingers through his hair. "Ezra doesn't have what it takes to be king. He never did. I'll get that mermaid to side with me, and we'll take the kingdom back."

What? I kept shaking my head, even though nobody could see me.

"Wait, so let me get this straight," the man said. "The mermaid is helping the island? If her time is running out, though, what use will she be?"

"I'll follow the same plan as Ezra," Tavo said, nodding.

What plan?

I was the glad the foreigner was confused as myself, because Tavo explained. "Ezra never planned on taking the mermaid to the sea because he wants to use her power to strengthen the land and heal the birds. He knows if he takes her to the sea, she'll swim away. She'll go back to her world. So he's determined to keep her here. Not because he loves her, but because he needs her gift."

My resilience faltered as Tavo continued. "Just her presence is healing the land. There are other forces at work that are killing it, like the frogs–"

And Cressida, I thought.

"... but that mermaid..." Tavo rubbed his chin thoughtfully again. "By the time she turns to sea foam, she would have brought the songbirds back to life, brought the trees back... It's a temporary fix, of course, but enough that the people will trust Ezra is doing good for them."

At this point, I should have called for Ezra in my mind, to tell him the lies his brother shared with this foreigner. But doubt crept in, like an eel sliding into a reef crevice.

What if? I swallowed hard. Ezra had not taken me to the ocean. He kept bringing it up, kept saying he wanted to... but what if Tavo was right? I had just... *trusted* Ezra. Had never questioned him.

But now I began to wonder.

Tavo and the man began walking away, speaking in quiet tones and leaving me in the bushes alone. I swatted at a bug biting my leg. Couldn't stand the itchy bug bites I was getting from standing here, but what choice did I have?

A shiver ran down my spine. I didn't believe Tavo... or, at least, I didn't want to. But I did begin to question... why hadn't Ezra taken me? He had a million reasons, and I excused him several times as well... but should I have done that?

And, suddenly, the world felt incredibly heavy. The weight of everything fell on my shoulders, as if a whale was sinking on me. *What if I can't trust Ezra?* Was he really just going to let me die?

He hasn't taken me to the sea... So... maybe? Tears welled up in my eyes and I ran to my room before they fell. I felt so lost... so terrified. In a world I didn't know, surrounded by people I thought I could trust and yet... I could not.

And, for the first time since leaving, I desperately wished I could be home: safe, in the underwater world, hidden from view of the outside, political, torrential world of the humans.

CHAPTER THIRTEEN
EZRA

The whole day was chaotic. It all started with a knock on my door, and Aulani calling me from the other side.

Ezra, Ezra! Hurry!

I scrambled to get ready, and when I found her in the hallway, pacing, she rushed to me. But she didn't embrace me. Instead she quickly told me about Cressida.

I felt magic last night, and I hurried to follow it. Cressida said a spell and it takes life from the island, but uses that magic to turn people into frogs.

I gaped. *Is she turning people into frogs?*

Who knows? Has anyone gone missing?

We've since located the missing noblemen and women, I said, then hurried to button my tunic and fix my sleeves. They went into hiding, afraid of what Cressida might do to them because they disagreed with her. I ordered my nearest guards to bring Cressida to the throne room for questioning.

And Ezra. Aulani's eyes did not have their usual glow to them, the one that said she was happy to see me.

Instead, she looked worn down, tired, like something worried her.

Yes? I took her hand and she forced a smile.

Are you going to take me to the sea today?

I promise it. And this time I meant it. I had broken too many promises to her. At that very moment, Hoʻohuli came bursting in.

"The frogs, your majesty. The hunters went out last night, but they said they're spreading faster than ever."

"What do you mean?"

Aulani eyed my counselor with suspicion, and when he nodded to her, she tipped her head, as if studying him.

"You mean to say there are *more* frogs?" I asked.

Hoʻohuli looked frantic. "Yes, sir. But people are saying parts of the forest are dying, while others are healing... and it seems the forest closest to the palace is healing. It's thriving even! But other parts of the island..." He shook his head. "If we don't do something, our island will die."

I met Aulani's eyes and she nodded. *We have to help, Ezra.* But it seemed like the coral walls in her mind had doubled overnight, and I couldn't even sense any underlying currents of her feelings.

"People are talking," Hoʻohuli added, and turned to the mermaid princess. "They're wanting *you,* Miss Aulani, to come to their villages and towns. You're a miracle to them."

"No," I said suddenly and sharply. "I'm taking Aulani to the sea today." A promise was a promise.

But the birds... She hesitated, even as she said it, and her gaze looked past me, to the distant sea, miles away.

"We're going to the sea," I said again, and Hoʻohuli let out a breath.

"Yes, your majesty."

Ezra. Aulani squeezed my hand. *What about your people?*

I've already asked enough of you–

The birds? The island? The trees? Not only has Cressida's magic negatively affected it, but how will you help them get their life back? Their desire? They need something more.

I hesitated. They needed Aulani. But I couldn't do that.

I can do it, she said. *For you.*

I shook my head.

This is my decision. Her intense gaze poured through me, and I knew nothing I said would change her mind. It touched me more deeply than she'd ever know.

"Alright, but I'm taking you to the sea," I reassured her. "Tonight."

"You can't go with her," Hoʻohuli said. "You're needed here, your majesty." He looked sympathetic. "Kalei can go with her to the villages and forests. We'll have them both back by the banquet tonight."

Ah yes. Another banquet. What was this one for?

The anniversary of my father's death. It was to honor him. I took a silent breath. If only father were here. He'd know what to do... about everything: Tavo. The birds. Aulani, even.

Call me if you need anything, I said, and she nodded.

I will.

Just then some guards came running down the hallway. "Your majesty," they said, out of breath. "Princess Cressida is missing. She was here last night but is nowhere to be found this morning. Her servants and guards won't answer questions."

I pursed my lips. *One more thing to add to the list.*

"Send out a search for her. I want her–and that golden ball–back in this palace by the end of the day."

"Yes, your majesty." The guards hurried out.

We'll keep an eye out for her, Aulani assured me, then left with Ho'ohuli. I stood there, alone, the garden quiet except for the faint rustle of leaves in the night wind. Usually, she'd turn back and give me that small wave, something to anchor me.

But this time, nothing.

The weight of the palace, the throne, my father's absence... it pressed down harder than any armor. Every decision, every expectation, every life depended on me... and I was supposed to lead. Should I even try? My thoughts spiraled. I wasn't ready. Maybe I'd never been ready.

Should I give the throne to Tavo? Let him take control of the island I'd grown to love? Our trees, our songbirds, our traditions... all at risk under his hands, under the foreigners' hands if he followed their ways.

But what if fighting for it was pointless? Had I already failed in ways I couldn't undo? A tight lump formed in my throat. I shook my head, trying to force the dark thoughts away. The island needed me. There were endless negotiations to plan, endless decisions to make. I had to keep moving, had to keep my hands in the soil of my people's land, even if my heart felt like it was slipping away.

THE DAY DRAGGED on like a snail crossing over a field of dirt. When the banquet finally arrived, I was relieved to see Aulani sitting at my right hand side, as usual. She didn't say much to my mind, and that worried me.

Things went well today, she said, but she was distant. Her eyes kept scanning the table, looking at Tavo then me, then the food. My brother ate with confidence and gusto, aware of the tension he was causing.

"We're honoring our father," I told him before the

banquet. "Let's try to act like we're friends for his sake. We don't want to dishonor his legacy."

Tavo laughed and nodded, but said, "What do you know of legacy, Ezra? All you're going to do is shatter what our forefathers started..."

But we didn't speak more because guests began arriving and we greeted them. Tonight there were more family members than nobles, and Kalei's entire family–including her parents and siblings–were also present.

If there was ever a time I felt more pressure in my place as king, it was now. Yet, everyone played their parts well. Tavo did not say one thing about politics or his foreign ideologies, but, instead, entertained the table with stories of his life in foreign lands. He had so many exotic tales, having seen so many things, I began to feel smaller and smaller.

When asked about Cressida, Tavo said things were rocky between them. "And, as you all probably know by now, she's under arrest for treason." He shrugged and eyed me. "My brother probably knows more about that. He's king, after all."

Want me to splash water on his face? Aulani's voice piped up in my head and, for a moment, I thought she was back. Back to teasing. Back to making me laugh. Instead, she only looked annoyed.

Maybe later.

The corner of her lip turned up and I was glad to have made her smile, if only a little.

After the dinner, we moved to the dance floor.

"Will you dance with me?" I asked Aulani and she nodded, taking my hand in hers. As we swayed together, it dawned on me...

This is it. Tonight she'd go to the sea.

The old man in the village hadn't been able to find a way for her to stay.

Nobody had.

So she'd find her realm tonight and call the sea to help her get back to it. I asked her to stay, tried to find a way for her to stay, but... there was nothing we could do. The sea witch's magic was too powerful. Unbreakable.

She had to go back and marry Prince Ryker, or she would die.

I held her a little closer to me, feeling her warmth, soaking in her salty, coconut beach scent, and wishing things were different. She rested her head against my chest, and I felt it: her longing, unspoken grief.

Our time is up.

And just as I thought that, a *pū* sounded, ringing loud and clear. Everyone stopped, the music faded, and all eyes turned to see Tavo with the conch shell, standing near the throne. He sat on it, folded his arms, and smiled at me.

"Now that all our family is here, I think it's about time they knew the truth, don't you Ezra?"

My blood went cold, though Aulani's hand in mine was warm.

"What are you talking about?"

Tavo spoke to the people. "Ezra does not have true islander's blood. And because he's not truly one of ours, he plans to do exactly what Cressida did, except in his own manipulative way." He leaned forward, loud enough so we all could hear. "He's going to close the island to foreign trade, and cut this land off from the outside world. As it grows stronger with weapons and technology, we grow weaker. And when we are weak, foreign powers take over us so easily, we have no way to defend ourselves. Ezra is making us vulnerable. There's a balance in all things, and he hasn't found it."

My stomach tightened. "That's not what I'm doing at all, Tavo. You know it. I'm negotiating with foreigners. We're going to allow them in, just with guidelines and restrictions."

"If we don't start trading and moving now," Tavo interrupted, "they're going to swoop in and take over." He was instilling fear in our people, in our family.

"We must honor the ways of our ancestors and respect the 'aina," I started, but Tavo was louder. He had always been louder.

"I take my rightful place as king." Gasps rippled through the crowd.

"You can't do that." I shook my head and nodded to my guards, but they hesitated. And that's when I realized... the room was being flooded with foreigners.

Tavo's army. My guards, now aware of the situation, remained loyal. They moved towards me, to protect me.

"I knew you'd put up a fight," Tavo said. "So I'm going to give you a choice, Ezra. Stand down and bow to me as your king, or get locked up with Cressida–once we find her."

Aulani looked around, at the windows. *Don't bow to him,* she said softly, though her mind seemed to be elsewhere, searching for something...

"Don't do it," Ho'ohuli said from the side.

I stood taller. "I am the king of this island, Tavo, and I am pushing for peace–both for our islanders and for the foreigners. You want to eradicate our forests and put our native people on the bottom of the pedestal. I can't do that."

"Then that is your choice." Tavo laughed and stood,

nodding to his men. "Take him!" And, just like that, chaos ensued. All the banquet-goers scattered like ants while my guards rushed to me. Tavo's men came running too, and screaming, shouting, and swords clashing filled the air.

This was not right. This was not how things should be done. I'd always been about the pen over the sword, but could words help me now?

A foreigner grabbed my arm, and I had no way to defend myself that night because I was unarmed. It was a stupid move on my part, but I figured we were honoring our father, the late king, and there would be no need for weapons.

If father saw what was happening now...

Tavo's troops overwhelmed my guards. There were too many of Tavo's troops flooding in, filling the whole room with their screams and shouts.

And then...

Music... It wasn't the music of instruments, but of nature. A wind gushed open the side doors, and, with it, a trail of colorful birds came flying in, Pili at the head.

It was a rainbow of colors and chaos.

The birds began attacking the foreigners, and it didn't take me long to realize that Aulani had summoned them.

"Stop!" I yelled, and the entire room went silent. The birds flew to the corners and Tavo and his men fled towards the door. "*Stop!*" I exclaimed again, chasing after my brother. "We can work together!" I was breathless. "You're my brother–" I began to say, but Tavo just laughed as he wiped sweat from his forehead.

"You were always too soft to rule." His expression hardened. "I will be king one day, Ezra, and you will see that gentleness does not win battles or kingdoms."

My stomach tightened.

"Come on!" Tavo and his men ran out. My guards were about to chase them when I raised my hand, halting them.

Why not? Aulani sounded amazed, and even Ho'ohuli let out a huff.

"This is treason–" he began, but I shook my head and he went silent.

The birds slowly trickled out of the room.

Finally, with Tavo and the foreigners gone, cheers rang out. But it wasn't for me. It was for Aulani. People rushed around her, showering her with kisses and hugs. They were so grateful, knowing that *she* had summoned the birds to protect me. To protect the throne.

And that was when I realized... *I have to let her go.* She had given everything–*everything*–to help me. And I could not keep her here any moment longer. She deserved to go home, to be with her kind, and to fall in love with the other prince.

I swallowed hard as I watched her, that radiant smile lighting up her face like the sun dancing over the Kaiora cliffs. And for the first time, I realized how painfully human my heart felt... how much it wanted something I could barely reach.

Not just for her. For us. For the life we might have had if the tides had been different.

I was not enough for her—not yet. But I would be... by taking her to the sea and letting her go.

CHAPTER FOURTEEN
AULANI

Ezra's strong arms held the reins as we rode to the beach together. After the scenario with the foreigners and the birds had died down, he spared no time preparing the open carriage and bringing me to the sea. I told him he had better stay to make sure Tavo was found and didn't wreak any more havoc, but Ezra was determined.

We rode for a long while before the water sparkled before our eyes.

My heart lightened, especially since I knew what would happen once I touched the water. I wouldn't turn back into a mermaid, but I'd be able to see where my home was. And once I knew that, I could summon sea creatures to help me get home.

Home. A lump formed in my throat. Was it home without him?

What about Humu and Mo? Wouldn't I be happy to see them, and them to see me?

The king's hands held my waist as he helped me dismount. Ezra had been unusually quiet, and the koa tree walls in his mind were extra sturdy. Did I do something wrong? Was I too much?

Probably. I'd always been too much for everyone, a reality that began to sink in deeper and deeper. And because I was too much, I didn't belong.

I never did. I had to leave. Ezra's island was doing much better, especially after Kalei and I went to the worst spots and I sang to the birds and trees in my mind.

But I had to get home.

For a moment, Ezra didn't take his hands off my waist. He looked into my eyes, his green ones swimming in grief. I offered a small smile, then walked towards the water. The smell of salt and the sound of the crashing waves filled the air. Nostalgia, which I had bottled up, finally came loose because I hadn't been here in so long.

Ezra waited back, watching as I touched the water. I stepped in, feeling it swirl around my ankles. Shaking my head, because it did not feel familiar, not even a strand of it, I went in deeper, until I finally submerged myself under it.

The water here was warm and crystal clear, even in the moonlight. My hair floated around me and I listened. Felt. Sensed.

The currents were not strong here, and the waves were calm. I expanded my mind, moving past coral reefs, large whales, distant islands, and sandy beaches hundreds of miles away. I searched for the Coral Realms, the Pearl Realms, even the briney depths where King Malinoakea lived.

But there was nothing.

No mermaids. No underwater kingdoms. I reached out to the currents, begging them to tell me of underwater mermaid worlds, but they shrugged me off. The fish darted away, not used to their minds being touched by one like me.

The water did not pull me home, just as it did for all mermaids who swam too far.

This is not my sea.

And it didn't even connect to my sea.

That's when it hit me like tumbling down a wave.

I'm not going home, I whispered, my breaths shallow and short. *Ezra... I'm not going home. It's not connected. This is not my sea. This isn't my world...* I wasn't crying, I was panicking, my blood rushing, my heart racing.

Ezra held me as I shook. "Then this is home," he said, but I turned away and shook my head, grabbing my hair and looking around.

I'm going to die, Ezra. I felt it closing in: turning to sea foam, all alone in a world that wasn't mine...

What have I done? I raced to the shore and began pacing.

"Aulani." Ezra approached but I pushed his hand away, my thoughts swimming faster than a fish escaping a shark. "It's going to be alright."

It's not going to be alright... My sea. My home. It was not here. And because there was absolutely no way to get back, I was going to die.

I never should have left... never should have taken the potion...

"Aulani..."

No, Ezra! Please! I stood before him, and that's when tears stung my eyes, causing him to blur before me. *Please give me a moment. Go back to the palace and take care of things. I just... I need to be alone.*

Because this was breaking me. Us. His expression fell and he nodded, stepping back.

I watched as he walked away along the beach, his footsteps in the sand, washed away by the waves.

I don't belong here. I don't belong anywhere–not the ocean, not this world, not beside Ezra. I swiped my hands through my hair and fell to the sand. *And because I thought I could belong somewhere–because I thought things were better elsewhere, I lost everything.*

Then the thought returned, one that kept repeating itself over and over in my mind, an image of sea foam floating on the water's surface. *And I'm going to die...*

CHAPTER FIFTEEN
EZRA

Mud caked my shoes as I picked up debris and rocks with each step back to the palace. But it hadn't rained, so the roads were clear and the moon shone down on it. Coquis chirped loudly and my heart sank even further. As if it couldn't go any further.

Aulani's sea is not connected. So there was no way to get her home. And if there was no way to get her to Prince Ryker, then she was going to die.

This is all my fault. If we had discovered this sooner, could we have found some portal, some magical way to get her back to her world? This is how she got here. Who opened the portal for her anyways?

When I reached the palace, Kalei and Hoʻohuli waited for me, and, upon seeing me without Aulani, tears streamed down Kalei's face.

Hoʻohuli let out a sigh. Perhaps he'd hoped I would marry Aulani, and that we'd rule together.

But it wasn't meant to be. I spoke, my voice low, full of sorrow. "She's still here," I said.

"Wait... she didn't go home?" Kalei wiped her eyes.

"Her home isn't connected to ours so..." I didn't finish and I didn't need to. Kalei's eyes widened and Ho'ohuli quickly said, "There must be someone here who knows magic... someone who can open a portal..."

A lump formed in my throat and I shook my head, wanting nothing more than to be alone in the terrace garden under grandfather's kukui tree.

"We tried that," I said and walked off, rubbing the back of my neck, wishing there was more I could do for Aulani... and, well, for *us*. I had hoped we could find a way for her to stay.

But I'm never doing enough. Never coming up with enough solutions. Never following the journey in the way tales should go. It seemed everyone else got a happily-ever-after and ruled so peacefully and well. But I? *I'm just not quick or wise enough.*

I never had been. I sat under the kukui tree and listened to the breeze rustle through the leaves. It seemed unfortunate circumstances always befell me: losing my older brother and becoming King, becoming a frog and losing my father during that time, falling in love with a mermaid only to find out she would die–and it was my fault because I didn't get her to the sea sooner–and now? Well... now my throne was about to be taken from me if my brother had things his way.

I put my head in my hands and sighed. When would I ever do things right? When would I ever be enough for my kingdom, my people, and even for myself? Not only did I mess up, I ruined everything. *Everything.*

Tavo would probably take over. Aulani was going to die. Cressida... well, she was on the loose and probably using her magical ball to destroy my island...

Another breeze blew through the leaves and, in my darkest moment, I thought I heard something.

Ezra...

I perked up. Did someone say my name? Looking around though, I was all alone.

I shook my head.

I was delirious. Too absorbed in my grief to think straight. But then I heard my name again, and I looked up at the silver undersides of the leaves.

You are the king... chosen by the people. Chosen by the island. The voice was gentle, like moss growing softly over stone, yet old and weathered like the cliffs carved by wind and waves. And it was then I realized. It was no ordinary voice.

It was my grandfather's voice. For so many years, I sat under this tree, hoping, maybe even praying that his wisdom might befall me. And here it was.

"Chosen by the people? I was just the spare," I whispered, but the leaves rustled, as if shaking their heads at me. Then it dawned on me.

Yes, the truth is that I was a spare. I was the one that people didn't think would ever become king. Yet, they did choose me after Tavo's death. I remembered when the news spread that I was to become king, and people congratulated me. It was always with sadness, because my brother died, but they had confidence in me.

And, beyond that, the island depended on me. Because of me, the frog problem was being taken care of. Foreigners were coming in, yet they were not devastating the land. Our people were still thriving, despite all the plantations and other goods that were going to be traded and would affect the land.

I'm not Tavo.

Tavo wanted to change everything and destroy our land, our traditions, and our culture. But I came in with a different approach: to blend it all, to embrace it all, while still preserving our roots.

Roots. Yes, that was it. Father had told me time and again that this island didn't need another Tavo. It needed me, and I'd done my best so far.

And I'll keep doing my best. I wasn't the king that my people had always imagined and thought would be their king, but I was going to fight for them, no matter what.

And I'm going to fight for Aulani. I was not the prince she was supposed to fall in love with, but I loved her. This wasn't the way the tale was supposed to go, the trajectory that was set out for us, but one could transform their own tale, right?

Hadn't we done that so many times while we were together? We'd found a way to communicate. She healed the birds, and I healed her heart. We belonged together. There had to be a reason we, from two different worlds, found each other.

I stood, my mind made up. We probably had a few days left to figure things out with Aulani's curse, but I'd do everything in my power... even if it meant finding the one person I knew could do magic, the one person who could transform others...

CHAPTER SIXTEEN
AULANI

I sat on the beach crying for so long that the sea salt had dried and my clothes and hair felt sticky and stiff. I wiped my eyes and sniffed, looking up at the stars and the moon.

I traded my underwater life for a sight I could see from the sea. I didn't need a telescope to see more. I could enjoy the view I had...

But I've always wanted more. I felt I was meant for greater things, and being different from the other mermaids didn't help. None of them communicated with the animals and living plants as deeply as I did. So it seemed right that I had to leave.

I thought I belonged in the human world. And now I knew that I did not. Ezra had kept his promise and brought me here, but even he could do nothing for me. I had tangled myself in this mess, thinking I could belong here.

I'm only going to turn to sea foam now...

Pili swooped down and landed on my shoulder. He let out a soft sound, as if aware that I was sad and grieving. He nudged his soft head against my cheek and I stroked his red feathers. Now that he perched on my hand, I couldn't help but admire just how beautiful he was. All of the songbirds were beautiful, and their songs? Even more beautiful. I would miss them.

I'll miss everything. I'll miss him. Because soon, I'd be nothing.

For another long moment, I listened to the waves breaking on the shore. The sea was loud, but it wasn't annoying or pesky like the coqui frogs from the nearby forest.

They don't belong here, I thought. They were an invasive species, causing endless noise pollution and eating all the bugs so the native birds starved to death. And then it dawned on me... the coqui frogs did *not* belong here, yet, somehow, I did.

Because of me, the songbirds were thriving again. Because of me, we'd find Cressida's magic ball and stop the leeching of the island's life. I also thwarted Tavo and his crew's attempt to steal the throne from Ezra.

I remembered telling Aunty Lorelei that I wanted to come here because maybe–just maybe–it was my calling. She said curiosity was not the same as calling, but it was not just curiosity. Perhaps I *did* have something to offer here.

I looked at the forest in the distance, and my eyes narrowed. A thin pillar of smoke rose into the sky, a sign that someone was setting up camp there.

And I knew who it was.

Tavo said he was going to start chopping down trees. He even had the crew ready to do it. He even had his fleets ready to ship off the wood...

I can't let him do that.

My fists clenched at the thought of him destroying the

forest. Ezra would *never* do such a thing... and my heart skipped a beat.

It's why I love him so much.

Love? I almost laughed aloud at myself. *Of course I love Ezra!* But I was terrified to admit it because, well, I was supposed to fall in love with Prince Ryker. I never really wanted to from the beginning.

He was a means to discovering the human world, and I hated that I wanted to just use him.

I couldn't do that to him. And I wouldn't. Besides, I had no access to my world.

As if a whisper from the sea, I heard a voice: *You will need to win the right prince's heart to stay.*

The right prince's heart? That was the terms of the spell that transformed me.

I gaped.

Prince Ryker was not the right prince for me.

He never had been.

But with Ezra, it was different... vastly different. I wanted to fall in love with him so I could stay... not just in his world, but *with him.* He was everything I wanted and needed: grounded, rooted, steady. I moved and bubbled with every current of emotion and whim, but he did not move, and I loved him for that.

And, in that moment, I realized that if I was going to die and turn to sea foam, I might as well show my love for Ezra by doing everything I could to help him save his kingdom, once and for all. I might as well do what I could to help eradicate the frogs, revive the birds, and bring the trees back to life. My time was running out.

As I stood and dusted myself off, I smiled at the sea, grateful. Happy, even, despite my doom coming for me faster than a tsunami, swallowing the shore whole.

There was a time I despised being a mermaid, especially being *me,* but now I knew better, and my aunt's words came into my ears. It felt as if I were in her arms now as she comforted me after receiving the news of my betrothal to the king of the brine.

You can stay, use your gifts, love bravely, and be exactly who Akua made you to be — both ocean and land, past and future.

Yes, I was all of those things! All of those wonderful things.

I gasped.

Now I had work to do. One last way to use my gifts, love bravely, and be exactly who I was meant to be. I was not just ocean, but I was land. I wasn't just my past, but the future. And if I wanted Ezra to know how I really felt, and if I was going to use my gifts in the calling I never realized I had, then I had to act now.

I hiked up my skirts and began running across the sandy beach, towards the nearest forest and the plume rising into the air.

I'm going to stop Tavo and help the island, I thought. *Even if it was the last thing I did.*

As if in response, the sea surged and a wave rushed past my feet. The saltwater was refreshing, warm, and comfortable. Perhaps it wasn't my sea, but I was grateful for it.

This is not how I thought things would end, I told myself, then smiled because in the end, I got to choose the new tale–the transformed tale.

CHAPTER SEVENTEEN
EZRA

It was morning by the time my guards found Princess Cressida. Word also reached me that Tavo had taken his troops into the Wailea forest, where he was already setting up camp and preparing to chop down the trees.

While my men prepared their horses and weapons for battle, I took a moment to storm down into the prison. My guards had finally found her, and I was ready to confront her.

Princess Cressida waited patiently, her belongings in a box far from where she could reach it.

“When my father hears that you’ve put me in prison, you’ll pay for it.”

“Good morning to you too,” I said and went straight for her belongings. As I dug through her bag, my skin stood on edge as I found what I’d been looking for: the golden ball.

Aulani was right.

“You’ve been stealing life from the land for this magic thing,” I said and she frowned.

“That’s a ridiculous idea–”

"Aulani found you doing it, so don't lie to me."

She froze, her face turning pale, before she leaned against the prison bars and said softly, "So that *was* her the other night."

"Yes, and you're going to tell me how to use this thing."

Cressida laughed. "You don't know the first thing about magic, do you Ezra?"

"No, but you're going to tell me. Can this transform someone permanently into a human?"

Her eyebrows creased. "There is always a price."

"What is the price?"

"True magic always takes something in return, remember? This ball can only take from the natural life here, including the plants and people."

"People?"

"Transforming someone permanently into a human would require a great deal of magic. It would suck the island dry."

My throat felt dry at that thought. "What if it took from me?"

"There is the possibility of performing a swap," she said, then leaned over. "What are you trying to do?"

"Transform Aulani into a human permanently. She's a–"

"Mermaid. Yes, Tavo told me."

"Tavo?" I gaped. "Who told Tavo?"

She hesitated, and, instead of answering, said, "Tavo has had his secrets, Ezra."

I frowned. "And you've been in on them all along, haven't you?"

"No." Cressida quickly grew defensive. "No, not at all... Well, not since he first left." She shook her head and let out a breath. "He's changed, alright? And so have I."

This time, I hesitated. What was I doing trusting Cressida? She turned me into a frog... *twice!* And now I wanted her to do magic again? What if she did something wrong?

"Did you and Tavo have plans of your own?" I asked, remembering our walk in the garden, remembering how she wanted to carry on his legacy.

The princess looked away, her expression almost embarrassed. "Yes. I thought he was in love with me. Before he left, he told me that our bond would strengthen foreign alliances. He had so many ideas, Ezra. They sounded so grand, and..." She sighed. "For once, I thought I could be part of something. Thought I was actually good for something and could rule by his side. He blinded me... then he never came back. But..." She pursed her lips. "I was sure he hadn't died–I could feel it. Then it dawned on me: he abandoned me." Her fists clenched. "So I am sorry Ezra. I did what I thought would turn the tables in my favor. I was desperate, and then he did come back. I was right. He had plans of his own... and they did not involve me."

I froze. All along she thought Tavo was good, and that he really wanted to help Kaiora. She thought she could play a huge role in that.

Turns out he lied.

"He lied to all of us," I said, and swallowed hard.

We stood in silence for a moment, then Cressida said, "I can transform Aulani into a human permanently, but there are limits to my magic."

"What are the conditions?"

She rubbed her forehead. "Listen, if you transform, you can permanently transfer your human life to something else, turning it into a human forever."

I gaped. "So you could permanently change me into a frog, and Aulani would stay human forever?"

“Yes.”

I love her. But what about my kingdom? What about the island?

It will do better with her. Yes. I would give the kingdom to Aulani, make her ruler, and transform permanently into a frog.

The people love her. They adored her, and, even without a voice, her presence was enough for them. She would rule well. I made up my mind. Aulani could not turn to sea foam. I’d do *anything* for her.

“Come on,” I said, grabbing the keys and giving Cressida a look. “Do I have your word you’ll help me follow through with this?”

She tipped her head. “One condition.”

“What is that?”

“If I transform you into a frog and transfer your permanent human life to Aulani, I want to live here. Punish me here–I’ll do whatever it is to make amends for my wrongs, but don’t send me to Windmere.”

“Why?”

Cressida looked away, as if embarrassed. “I do not wish to return home, Ezra.”

“You can’t live here,” I said. "I will put you on trial for everything you did to me, the people, and Kaiora, and then I will send you back."

“*Please*... can my punishment be here? I will never do magic again, just... don’t send me to my family.”

I frowned. She made our lives miserable, so why not make hers miserable?

“I’m sending you back to Windmere.”

Her fingers wrapped around the iron bars. “I feel I could start new here, Ezra. If I go home... father will just... betroth me to someone else, and I do not want it. It's been a nightmare with Tavo, then you, and Tavo again..."

For whatever reason, I felt sorry for Cressida. We came from similar backgrounds: the spares to the throne, except I became king and she was still tossed around for marriage like a leaf blowing in the wind.

No wonder she tried to turn the tables in her favor after Tavo's death.

I said, "You must stand trial first. Then I will send word to your father. If he agrees to your punishment here, you will stay and be loyal to this crown and kingdom forever. If not, you will go."

"I understand." She nodded, a little relief crossing her face. "I just hope he will not request me to come home."

Home. It was a word we all tossed around. Aulani was trying to get home. Cressida was trying to flee home. Tavo was trying to take over his home. And I? Well... I was trying to protect my home. I was trying to protect *her.*

"Come on," I said, unlocking the door, then paused as Cressida stepped out. Our eyes met and she sighed, holding out her hand.

"Ezra, I really am sorry for changing you into a frog," she said, and I hesitated before shaking it.

"My father died trying to find me," I said, and she visibly cringed.

"Yes, and I am truly sorry for that too... I suppose this is the best way I can repay you... by helping you save the girl you love."

I nodded and an understanding passed through us. I shook her hand. This was a new beginning, a fresh start for the "spares" in their kingdoms. But we were spares no longer.

CHAPTER EIGHTEEN
AULANI

I walked through the forest, unafraid to be seen. Morning light danced through the trees, and I could hear the ocean waves not far from here. The birds began circling above, and the bugs, plants, flowers, and insects seemed to respond to my plea for help. I could feel them prepared to stand in solidarity with me, even to fight.

We must stop Tavo, I told them. *He's going to hurt the island.*

The campfire smoke grew stronger the closer I got, and, soon, I heard men talking, metal grinding, and axes hacking.

Already at work. I shook my head to myself, saddened that Tavo had turned against the island and his people.

"Whoa! Look who's here!" A man called out and Tavo appeared, his shirt off, sweat dripping down his big, bulky frame.

"Ah, Aulani." He grinned. "Come to join me? You're a little late, dear. My offer to you and my brother has expired."

I shook my head, and he frowned, as if realizing I was

completely alone. It was a strange thing. And then... "Did you call on all those birds last night?" He gaped. "It's you..."

Before he could rally his men to snatch me, I nodded and, from all around me, the leaves began shaking in the branches. The trunks swayed, and just the noise from the movement spooked the men.

Leave, I wanted to tell Tavo, but some of his men already dropped their tools and stepped back, looking from the trees to me.

A man reached out and grabbed my wrist, dragging me towards Tavo. I tried to resist, pushing him away. Then, something happened. The *frogs* responded to my call. I had never reached out to them, bothered by them as I was, but I could feel them *worrying* for me...

Help me! And suddenly frogs came from every direction, jumping onto the man who grabbed my wrist. He let go immediately, trying to swat at the frogs jumping all around him.

"We can't keep doing this!" exclaimed one of the men and they all scurried away. Tavo was furious, watching his crew disappear.

"You cowards!" he cursed at them. "Come back! *Come back!*"

And, soon, it was just Tavo and I in the clearing. He seethed with anger, looking at all the abandoned tools and tents. "This is all your fault!" He grabbed a knife and marched towards me. "You filthy little mermaid! You–"

"That's enough." A new voice sounded as Ezra and Cressida came running through the bushes. Hoʻohuli also followed, along with several guards.

I looked from Ezra to Cressida, a wave of insecurity passing over me. Why were they together?

"Listen," said Tavo, now turning to Ezra. "It would be *so*

simple if you just gave me the throne. It was rightfully mine–"

"Until you faked your death," Ezra interrupted.

Tavo's nostrils flared and his eyes darted towards a figure that moved in the shadows, her steps hesitant.

Kalei?

"Kalei told me everything," Tavo laughed.

"I didn't want to," Kalei quickly replied, her face red. "He forced me to–"

"That's enough." Tavo grabbed her and held the knife to her throat. We all gasped, and I braced myself to call the birds.

But Ezra intervened, as if he read my thoughts. Probably did.

"Don't," he said softly to me.

But Ezra!

His attention was on his brother. "She's our *cousin,* Tavo. She's *family,*" said Ezra. "The people here. This island. Don't just turn against it all." He stepped forward, and my insides tightened. What was he doing? Now was not the time for diplomacy! But Ezra was sure of himself, more so than he'd ever been.

"Tavo. We can *still* work together. You're my brother–"

"Your half brother," Tavo spit. "If anything, Kalei should've taken the throne before you, Ezra. You're just a mutt–a half blood. You don't deserve the throne. You *never* did!"

Ezra's face paled, but only for a moment.

I reached out with my mind. *What is he talking about?*

My mother was a foreigner. Father married her after Tavo's mother passed away. My mother disappeared...

My heart ached for him. For Tavo. For their father. So much loss!

"I'm so sorry," Kalei whimpered. "I didn't want to tell him, but he told me if I didn't, he'd kill you Ezra..."

"Let. Her. Go." Ezra took a step and Tavo pressed his knife again. Kalei screamed.

"Give me the crown. Now." Tavo then turned to Ho'ohuli. "And you. Do the coronation words now."

The old man hesitated, and, with his hesitation, everyone seemed to hold their breaths. Tavo's expression hardened. "What are you waiting for old man?" He motioned to one of his men. "You! Get him to say the words!"

But even Tavo's crew was still.

Silent.

All eyes turned to Ezra, and there was nothing but respect. He had not forced his brother to do anything. Hadn't even physically fought him.

And they respected him for that.

I finally realized that Ezra's gentleness *was* his greatest strength. That no, he did not have to use brute force or power to influence his people or his kingdom. By giving people the power to choose–and yet still offering compassion–he had won this war.

It had never been a physical battle, despite what I'd believed.

"Let her go, Tavo," Ezra said once more. Then he turned to the others.

Ho'ohuli stepped forward. "The king may not fight you, Tavo," he said. "But we will fight on his behalf. He has asked for peace, extended compassion to you as your brother. You have only instigated violence and oppression."

More silence.

Ezra spoke up now to Tavo's men. "Join me and my people," he said. "We can work together in peace. Create alliances with foreign kingdoms that mutually benefit and respect us both."

The silent devotion shifted, like tides changing. Tavo's men could see the difference between Ezra and his brother.

Tavo gaped. "What are you waiting for?" he exclaimed, but his men did not move.

"We weren't looking for violence," said one of the foreigners, and threw down his weapon. The others followed.

And Tavo, now realizing his own defeat, released Kalei.

I rushed to grab Kalei and pull her back while Ezra's guards cuffed Tavo's large wrists. The man didn't even resist, accepting his loss respectfully.

"You're under arrest for treason," Ho'ohuli said. As the guards took Tavo past Ezra, the king let out a breath.

"I *am* sorry that things ended like this, Tavo. You're my brother, and I love you. I only hoped you would love our people the way I do. The way father did."

"Well I'm Tavo." He spit. "I do things differently." And with that, the guards took him away.

I finally turned to Ezra, ready to embrace him when...

What is she doing?

Cressida held out her golden ball, golden magic swirling around it. Ezra let out a breath and I gasped.

Ezra, no! She's turning you back into a frog!

Before I could leap towards Cressida to stop her, Kalei grabbed my arm.

"Stop, Aulani!"

No!

Ezra looked at me, the magic moving like ribbons around him. He let out a gasp and crouched down.

Ezra! I tried to break free of Kalei. However, Ezra spoke with a pained expression.

"Ho'ohuli knows this, but I give the crown to you, Aulani. You are queen of Kaiora–"

No. No!!!

You deserve to live, Aulani. His voice was tender, and he even smiled at me.

It all happened so quickly.

NO! Pili pecked Kalei's wrist and she let me go. I ran to Cressida, shoving her to the ground. Then I grabbed the ball, but the magic was still swirling.

Whatever spell she cast had been activated, swirling between Ezra and I... and if I didn't act quickly, Ezra would turn into a frog within seconds.

I grabbed the nearest hard object I could find: an ax. And with that, I let it drop on the ball. I had surprisingly good aim, because it landed right in the center of the sphere. As soon as it hit, golden light exploded all around us and I flew backwards.

"Aulani!" It took a moment before Ezra came running towards me, cradling me in his arms. "Aulani, why did you do that? You were supposed to live. The spell would make me transform into a frog, but you would be human forever." Now tears stung his eyes.

I blinked a few times, then touched his soft cheek. *You are the king here, Ezra. Don't croak on me now.*

Aulani, I'm serious.

I know. So am I. And then I kissed him, hoping he knew how much I loved him, and how I wanted things to be like this. Sure, the golden ball was our last chance to help me transform into a human forever, but it was not worth Ezra being a frog for life.

It had to be one or the other, me or him.

And I wanted him to live a long, full life. I had made my decision long ago when I took the potion from my aunt, and though I wished we could live happily ever after, I was content with this being the end: seeing Ezra as king, his brother locked away, the island returning to its former beauty.

Look, I said, pulling away and pointing to a spot in the clearing. The frogs assembled, hopping into a neat little pile. *They listen to me too,* I said, and Ezra gaped. I squeezed his hand.

I think we've figured out your frog problem. And, just like that, the frogs listened to me, congregating so that it was easy for the guards to put them in a container and ship them out of here.

Ezra let out a breath and hugged me. *Thank you, Aulani.* And I was grateful–so very grateful–to be able to help him. To serve him. To serve this island and people. And I wouldn't trade it for the world... not even my own world.

CHAPTER NINETEEN
EZRA

Aulani was all smiles as she hugged me tightly.

I tried to smile back, but it wasn't there. Everything was right, and yet... it was not right.

I held her hands, staring into her bright brown eyes until...

"Alright you two, break it up already."

We did so to see Kalei, and tears filled her eyes when she looked at me. "I'm so sorry Ezra. I should have never–"

"Kalei." I embraced my cousin.

She sobbed. "Tavo cornered me–"

"I know." Because I did know. Knew what it felt like to feel small, powerless, like nobody could help me. My time as a frog had done that, but, more so, being Tavo's younger brother made me feel what Kalei probably felt.

"And what he said... about the throne..." She wiped her tears and Aulani put her hand on Kalei's back. "You know I don't want it, right Ezra?"

"Kalei." I laughed. "You have supported me and been my friend since we were young. I know you would never try to hurt me." I gave her another hug. "Let's move on, alright?"

She nodded and hugged me back. "Thank you Ezra." Then, after a moment, she pulled away and punched my arm playfully. "You still ought to give your cousin a punishment though–for disloyalty to the throne. It's only fair and right."

A grave expression crossed my face. She was right. It was only fair. I couldn't show favoritism, not even to my favorite cousin. "You're right, Kalei. A fair trial will be held."

Aulani joked. *Perhaps she can serve as Kaiora's royal event coordinator as punishment. We know how much she loves balls.*

I voiced Aulani's words aloud and this time, Kalei laughed.

We hardly had a moment to joke around more because Aulani's expression changed and she suddenly looked away.

Someone is calling my name. The voice is familiar... She gazed at the sea, and then... she was running. Dashing towards the beach.

"Aulani!" I followed, and Hoʻohuli, Kalei, and Cressida followed too. The mermaid was so fast, that when she reached the water, it seemed to sparkle at her touch. The water swirled around and around until...

A woman emerged from the sea, a golden triton in her hand. I gaped, unable to stop staring at her green colored scales, iridescent tail, and bright green eyes. She looked familiar... so very familiar...

Before Aulani reached her, the woman stared at me, her mouth slightly open.

"Ezra?" she asked, and Aulani turned around.

You know Aunty Lorelei?

Lore... My head was spinning. Father spoke of his "dear Lore," who he missed everyday...

"It's my..." A lump formed in my throat and Aulani grabbed my hand.

Is she your mother, Ezra?

I nodded, putting all the pieces together. Somehow, this mermaid came to our world before. Walked among our people. Saved the birds. Married my father. Had me. And then she disappeared.

Because she returned to her world. Unlike Aulani...

"Ezra?" Her voice was the same one my father had described, soft yet unyielding.

I nodded, words failing me. My mother—*my mother*—stood before me. The woman who had walked through legends and gossip, the one who had saved the birds in the past, was here.

"My son..." Lorelei rose, eyes glistening, like she wanted to hug me but also hesitated. That hesitation caused my chest to squeeze. Did she not approve of me? Instead, she said, "We will reunite later, Ezra. For now... time is of the essence." She turned to Aulani, and that made me even more anxious. Was the mermaid's month up? Would she turn to sea foam?

"Oh, my dear..." The queen's expression softened. "You are *so* close to breaking the spell and remaining a human forever."

Aulani frowned, as if to ask, "How?"

Lorelei moved her triton, and light seemed to shimmer from the ends of it. She wove it in the air and again, there was a large gaping hole where once was nothing. Yet, inside of that hole shone a beautiful sea, and, in the distance, a castle with red shingles and white walls.

A portal. I stared, unable to process all of this.

Prince Ryker's castle... I blinked.

Aulani seemed confused, looking from the portal to her aunt. And then it dawned on me: this was Aulani's chance to go home. She could go to that castle *right* now, meet Prince Ryker, and possibly fall in love, which would allow her to live on as a human.

Because if not... I glanced at the sea foam floating on the distant waves.

"You may return home," Lorelei said, adding, "When you fled that night, your father and I pursued you. He drew on the magic of the triton, and I drew on ancient, unstable magic. It has been years since I drew on that well of magic, but I opened the portal, hoping it would be your escape. When your father couldn't find you, he turned to me for help." She held out the triton. "You will recognize this as an old triton, which your father gifted to me. It stabilizes ancient magic and has allowed me to create this portal." She tipped her head. "Your father could not come, in case our magic mixed and something terrible could result. This was the only way to ensure your safe passage back home."

Home... Aulani's home. My breath hitched.

Aulani froze in place. I wanted to reach out to her with my mind, but what was I to say?

Lorelei held the triton out for us to see. "Only I have the power to open the portals between worlds. Your father's triton cannot draw on the same magic that I can. He has allowed me my use of magic... in exchange for an offer to bring you home." She smiled.

The mermaid princess was still stuck in place, speechless.

Aulani? I finally reached out and she replied almost instantly.

My father... allowed Aunt Lorelei her magic... for me?

Yes, he did it for you, I confirmed. A tear slowly trickled down her cheek.

He did love me... albeit in his own complicated way.

And he wants you home, I said, though it pained me to do so... I didn't want her to leave. Didn't want any of this... but she had a chance to survive. She would meet Prince Ryker and follow the plan and story that had been prepared for her all along.

"Will you come home now, Aulani?" Aunty Lorelei asked, pointing to the portal.

All attention turned to the mermaid-turned-human. I could sense her thoughts racing, like leaves in a typhoon.

Then she looked at me, and a calm filled her mind.

Peace.

Aulani took my hand and squeezed it.

You have to go, I said softly. *Or you'll turn to sea foam...*

She smiled, not a hint of fear or doubt in her eyes. Not even hesitation. *I've made up my mind. You're the prince–now king–that I've chosen. You're right for me.*

My heart melted. It was her. Always her, but I would rather her live on. *I can't let you do this...*

I love you, she said and drew closer to me, the water swirling around us. I looked into her eyes, knowing there was nobody else I'd rather be with. Nobody else I could ever love as much as her...

I love you too.

In that moment, so tender, something happened. Golden lights sparkled around us. Magic floated in the air, and it was so buoyant it felt like we were floating, if only for a moment.

Aulani took a breath and gasped, clutching her throat. "Ezra!"

I gaped. "You can talk–"

"Took you long enough to say it, Ezra! I waited ten tides and five eternities for you to say it–"

And I couldn't hold back any longer. I kissed her, and she wrapped her arms around my neck, kissing me back. "The spell... it's broken?" I asked aloud, pulling away, just to make sure.

She laughed and looked towards her aunt. "It is, am I right?"

The woman nodded, her eyes rimmed with tears. She opened her arms and Aulani let go of me to embrace her. "You did it," my mother said, then held her arm out for me to hug her too. I couldn't believe I was actually embracing my mother. I never imagined this day would come–never imagined I would ever meet her.

She pulled away and kept one arm wrapped around Aulani's shoulders."You really did it, Aulani. And you found the right prince for you."

"Oh he's the *perfect* prince–king–for me." Aulani wiped some tears and then held my mother's hands. "I can't believe father was willing to allow you to use magic... for me."

"He misses you," my mother said, her eyes sad. "He wishes he had never said those things, banned you, or betrothed you to the briney king." She squeezed Aulani's hands. "And he wants you home, dear. We all do." But her eyes moved past Aulani, to me. "But we cannot ask that of you."

"Can I visit?" Aulani asked, hope in her voice.

The queen softened. "As keeper of the portals, I *will* very well be using this triton, and a visit from you–both of you–would be splendid."

I let out a quiet breath of relief, one I didn't know I was holding. So Aulani *would* be able to go home. Perhaps not all the time, but she could see her family, make amends, and have peace and closure with it all. Lorelei gave her a shell necklace. "Call whenever you're ready to visit home. I'll always hear you, my sweet... daughter in law?" She kissed the top of Aulani's head then winked at me. I nodded.

Mother looked like she wanted to say more, but, instead, squeezed my hand. Her eyes reflected mine.

"We have much to discuss, Ezra, but..." A laugh escaped and it sounded so much like I imagined it, I just stared. "You have a lot to do too."

Yes...

She looked at all the others standing on the beach. "We will have *much* to catch up on," she told us and winked.

"I hope to see you again soon, Aunty Lorelei. Thank you," Aulani said. The women embraced once more, and then we all watched as the sea witch leaped into the portal. Her tail splashed in the water. The portal closed swiftly behind her, leaving us with a view of the sky, as if it had never been there.

Aulani let out a breath, turned, and smiled at me and the others on the shore. "I think that's enough excitement for one day," she said, and I knew I would never tire of hearing her voice. I was glad everyone could hear it now too. She squeezed my hand before hugging everyone. And, lastly, she wrapped her arms around my neck.

"You know," she said, her voice soft. "You once asked me to stay, and you clearly stated your intentions why."

I grinned.

"So..." She raised an eyebrow. "Are your intentions still clear–"

I kissed her. I didn't care if everyone was watching. She smiled through our kisses, and I quietly said, after I pulled away, "My intentions are very, *very* clear. I was gone the moment you *splashed* into my life, and if you aren't going to be my wife, I might as well turn back into a frog."

"Well," she said, pulling back and playing with my hair. "I'm planning to stay *and* be your wife. And if you don't like it, let *minnow.*" I shook my head but laughed. Her eyes lit up, my favorite thing in the whole world to see.

CHAPTER TWENTY
AULANI

Ezra truly was the best king Kaiora had ever seen. The land was healing and being restored under his stewardship and with my help, uniting western ways and people with the natives of the land. We were swiftly married and I became Queen Aulani of Kaiora.

It was *so* good to have my voice back. People from all over asked questions about the sea and the Coral Realms. I taught the locals how to sing to the birds, and we continued to tackle the frog problem. By the day of our wedding, not a coqui could be heard.

Meanwhile, Hoʻohuli remained Ezra's close counselor and advisor. Kalei was our trusted and good friend, and, despite her feeling like a traitor, we reassured her it wasn't her fault. We still loved and cared for her.

She underwent a fair trial and accepted her punishment as assistant to the royal event planner.

Princess Cressida's trial took a long time, as we had to gather witnesses and give her a fair hearing. As punishment, she needed to restore the land that she damaged. She literally had to work the earth, and, last I heard, she had become a rather strong farmer and botanist.

Her father sent an apology letter, but did not interfere with her punishment nor fight it to get her back home. It was a testimony to the fact that he did not truly care for her and I hoped, with time, she might heal and find peace here in Kaiora, working and tending to the land.

Tavo's "troops" peacefully and willingly returned to their home, with Ezra promising to forge stronger ties with their governments.

Tavo was exiled, a decision Ezra did not take lightly. Now, Tavo had to confront the foreign cultures he so readily embraced for the rest of his days, never to return to Kaiora.

Tavo, much to his credit, did not resist or mouth another bad word against his brother. If anything, guards and servants who escorted Tavo off the island mentioned that he spoke highly of Ezra, as if he truly admired him.

And I couldn't blame him. *I* admired Ezra. He balanced everything so well, keeping his people grounded in their culture, roots, and land, while still being open to foreigners and their modern ways.

I thought of this as I stood on the balcony and stared up at the stars.

Thank you, I said, admiring the vast space above. The sea sparkled in the distance. The cool night breeze gently blew my hair and sheer, soft blue night robe.

Warm arms wrapped around my waist and my husband kissed my neck. I giggled and touched his face.

"You look like you're thinking about something," he said softly.

"Do you hope it's you?"

Ezra grinned and held me tighter. "Maybe." He followed my gaze. "Do you miss it?"

I nodded. "Sometimes it feels so far, but... I have you." I placed my hands on his arms. It was especially nice that we could actually speak to each other... not in our minds, but with our voices.

"We've both changed, haven't we?" Ezra said quietly. "Not just in body, but in heart. In the way we see the world, in the way we see each other."

"Yes... I thought I had to leave one world behind. To become someone new, someone better. But now... I see how much I was meant to be here. With you. And my gifts... they were all for a bigger purpose."

"You were meant for me, and I was meant for you." He leaned in closer, his lips brushing against my cheek. "And now we're both home. Here. With each other."

I turned so I could see his beautiful green eyes. "You know... I never imagined my tale would end like this."

He laughed. "Your tale... or your tail?"

"Both."

His smile only widened."It hasn't ended, Aulani. It's just transformed." Then he leaned in and kissed me. I could recall the first time we kissed—not so long ago—when I still had fins and he had just transformed from a frog into a man. That kiss had been a breach, exhilarating and joyful, like a whale breaking through the surface, like dolphins spinning mid-air in sun-kissed spray.

But this one... this kiss was so much more.

It was an anchor. A promise. A new beginning. And I was done for.

When we finally pulled apart, I grinned against his mouth. "So... what now?"

He kissed my jaw and spoke against my neck, then pulled back enough so I could see the mischief in his eyes. "Now? We live hoppily ever after."

I groaned, but laughed into his warm, hard chest. “If you ever turn back into a frog, I am *not* kissing you for a third time.”

He held me tighter and chuckled. “Deal. I promise I’ll try not to... but only if you promise never to flounder on me.”

“Ezra...” I looked up at him as he wiggled his eyebrows.

“What? Too much?”

“Way too much–I thought that was my part. I’m the one who’s too much.”

“Hmm, I don’t remember. Maybe you can show me.”

I laughed and kissed him anyway, grateful that he loved me no matter if I was a crazy mermaid-turned-human who swam against the current, who looked at the world with big eyes and a curious heart, and who wore her heart on her sleeve... because I most certainly had sleeves now.

As our kiss deepened into something more, I smiled at what had become of us–a mermaid and a frog. This was no longer the end of a fairy tale, but the start of something far better–a life no longer displaced. It was a life that was finally fully our own... and no one had to croak or grow a tail ever again.

THE END.

MAHALO!

Aloha! 🌺

If you enjoyed this book, I'd be so grateful if you recommended it to a friend—word of mouth really helps authors like me.

Leaving a quick review on Amazon or Goodreads would also mean a lot. Reviews help other readers know what to expect and help me keep creating stories you love.

As a thank you, here is a bonus chapter–a little peek into Alan's reunion with her family. I hope you enjoy it!

Mahalo for your support and kindness!

❤️Lei

BONUS CHAPTER - EZRA

The ocean stretched before us like a living jewel, sunlight bouncing off the waves in a million glittering shards. I could feel Aulani's excitement even without the mind-link —it radiated from her like a warm current.

"Ezra! Look—Humu!" she cried, pointing toward the small fish darting near the shoreline. Even as a human, she had a way of drawing the sea to her, a quiet magic in her presence. "I'm telling you, this little guy has more personality than half the animals I've met!" she added with a laugh.

The fish swam around her, and, though I could not understand what Aulani might be communicating in her mind, I could tell that the fish was very excited. He splashed in and out of the water and darted in circles.

After their reunion, Humu swam back out to sea.

"The cove is right around here," Aulani said after a moment, taking my hand.

It had been a few months since we decided to come to Aulani's world together. When she blew into the seashell my mother gave her, a portal appeared and the sea witch asked if we were ready to come through.

We were.

And now we walked toward the cove, a secluded place where Aulani could reunite with her parents–away from the eyes of the humans. When we arrived, her parents waited at the water's edge, regal even with the sea breeze in their hair. Aulani paused, taking a deep breath.

"Mother... Father... I..." Her voice wavered, then steadied. "I'm sorry for running, for worrying you, for everything."

Her father's eyes softened. "Aulani, we should have trusted you more. You're not just our daughter—you're the heart of the Coral Realms, the keeper of the royal gardens, the girl who speaks to the animals. We should have listened sooner."

Her mother smiled, reaching for her hand. "We forgive you, Aulani. And we are proud of the woman you've become."

Aulani grinned and hugged her mother then her father. When she pulled away, she eyed her father. "Looks like we're even... but you better not expect me to stop asking questions about humans. I'm not trading curiosity for comfort." She tapped her temple. "Besides, I already know enough to start teaching the fish a thing or two about politics!"

I chuckled at her fire, feeling my chest swell. She belonged here, yet she had brought her home to me too.

Another mermaid appeared. "Mo!" Aulani embraced her sister, tears streaming down their cheeks. She'd told me all about Mohala and her betrayal, but Aulani harbored no ill feelings.

"I'm so, *so* sorry!" Mo said but Aulani shook her head.

"If it weren't for you, I wouldn't have Ezra. So thank you! It all worked out." She pulled away and held her sister's hands.

Mo laughed. "I was the villain in your tale, Au. I can't forgive myself–"

"Well you're going to have to, because your tale is just beginning." Aulani winked. "Aunt Lorelei says there are portals leading to other worlds that have never been explored."

Mo laughed. "I would never!"

"Maybe you'll accidentally splash into another world like me."

Her sister rolled her eyes, but Aulani's eyes were full of adventure. "You never know."

After warm embraces and laughter with her parents and sisters, Aulani leaned close and whispered, "I can't believe I'm back. Thank you for coming with me."

Kalei, who had come along and somehow disappeared behind us, caught up now, dark eyes wide with curiosity. "Do you think these humans have libraries to study too?" she asked, bouncing on her toes.

Aulani winked at me. "Looks like someone else is destined to make waves in another tale... maybe with a prince who collects books." I laughed softly, realizing there could be a story waiting for her in another world.

Then I heard my mother's voice, drawing my attention from my cousin and Aulani.

"Ezra," she said, stepping forward, eyes glistening. "My son."

I ran to her, feeling the months of worry and doubt melt away. She smelled faintly of sea salt and flowers. Somehow, this felt right. Somehow, we were here, together.

"I'm sorry I left when you were so young," she said. "I'd

returned here for a moment–only to check on my ailing mother–and that's when the king found out I'd used magic to leave. He did not allow me to leave ever again. I was heartbroken." Tears filled her eyes. "I wish I could have seen your father one last time, but I am happy I get to see you now."

We hugged and my heart ached for her. It was too bad that things had to be this way, but I, too, was grateful we had this moment together.

Later, Aulani and I paused on a cliffside overlooking the human kingdom's castle. Prince Ryker stood outside looking at the sea.

"Do you ever... wish things had gone differently? That you were meant to be there next to him instead of here?" I asked quietly.

She shook her head, eyes sparkling like sunlight on water. "No way... if I were here, you'd miss all my puns." She leaned closer, brushing her fingers through my hair, "I love having a king to annoy. You're all mine."

I laughed and put my hand on her waist. "You're never annoying. But you're all mine too." I felt like the luckiest man in two worlds.

Around us, the Coral Realms and sea kingdom hummed with life, laughter, and light. I looked at Aulani and felt it in my bones: home wasn't a place. It was wherever she was.

THE END.

ACKNOWLEDGMENTS

All the glory and thanks goes to God and Jesus Christ.

A huge thank you to Kayla Eshbaugh and Camille Peters for inviting me to the *Displaced Fairytales.* And thank you to everyone else in the group for all you've done. Each one of you contributed so much and I appreciate it: Annette, Abigail, Gabrielle, Sarah, Annabelle, and Mary! It's been a wild ride and I'm grateful for the opportunity to grow and challenge myself.

Thank you to my one and only, Jordan. I seriously couldn't have done this without you—I say it for every book but I really mean it with this book. Through the burnout, the discouragement, and the lows you supported me every step of the way and reminded me of what's most important. I love you so much and look forward to closing this chapter of writing and stepping into the next one, all thanks to you!!!

Thank you to my sweet daughters, plus one on the way. I love you all so much!

And, finally, a huge thanks to my wonderful readers and supporters. I hope this book encouraged and inspired you. Can't wait to share more stories with you soon, whether in this genre or another!

Much aloha!

ALSO BY LEIALOHA HUMPHERYS

The Incandescent Kingdoms Series

Married at Sunrise (A King Thrushbeard Retelling)

Hidden at Starshine (A Cinderella Retelling)

Stolen at Alpenglow (A Beauty and the Beast Retelling)

Cursed at Moonlight (A Rapunzel Retelling)

Enchanted at Fireblaze (A Sleeping Beauty Retelling)

Lost at Aurora (A Princess & the Pea Retelling)

Haunted at Twilight (A Hansel and Gretel Retelling)

Poisoned at Dawn (A Snow White Retelling)

These novellas take place in the Incandescent Kingdoms

Prequel Novella

Kidnapped at Dusk (A Red Riding Hood Retelling)

Download this prequel novella free at www.leialohahumpherys.com

The Shattered Tales

To Curse a Black Swan (A Swan Lake Retelling)

Autumn Fairy Tales

Filia and the Fall Festival (A Little Mermaid Retelling)

Hope Ever After

A Beautiful Hope (An Ugly Duckling Retelling)

Self Help

Aloha State of Mind

STANDALONE NOVELLAS

Falling for the Huntsman (A Villainous Twist on Snow White and Hansel & Gretel)

Transformed Tail (A Mashup of the Frog Prince and Little Mermaid)

Ghosts and Ginger Tea (Inspired by the Night Marchers)

ABOUT THE AUTHOR

Leialoha Humpherys writes stories anchored in Hawaii, heritage, and heart. Though she works across genres—from fantasy to reflective nonfiction—every story she tells is shaped by Hawaiian culture, island landscapes, and a deep love for home.

Raised on the Big Island of Hawaii and educated at the University of Hawaii at Hilo, Leialoha writes emotionally rich stories filled with resilience, hope, and belonging. She is the author of Aloha State of Mind and other works inspired by ancient Hawaii. Now living in Utah with her husband and children, she carries Hawaii with her—in her writing, her values, and every story she tells.

Follow her on social media and sign up for her newsletter at www.leialohahumpherys.com for updates and new stories!

DISPLACED FAIRYTALES

Want more no-spice fairy tale mash-ups? Check out the rest of the Displaced Fairytales multi-author collection!

Imprisoned Slumber (A Princess and the Pea and Sleeping Beauty Retelling) by Camille Peters

Transformed Tail (A Little Mermaid and Frog Prince Retelling) by Leialoha Humpherys

Burning Snow (A Little Match Girl and Snow Queen Retelling) by Abigail Manning

Beastly Dreams (A Sleeping Beauty and Beauty & the Beast Retelling) by Gabrielle Landi

Tangled Sails (A Rapunzel and Little Mermaid Retelling) by Annette Larsen

Cursed Climb (A Swan Lake and Jack & the Beanstalk Retelling) by Sarah Beran

Captured Crimes (A Goldilocks and East of the Wind, West of the Moon Retelling) by Anabelle Raven

Bluebeard's Bride (A Bluebeard and Aladdin Retelling) by Mary Mecham